THE SAINT AND THE TURTLE

JON P. GUNN

iCrew
digital publishing

OTHER BOOKS BY JON P. GUNN

The Apes of Eden Saga

The Journey Begins
The House of Solomon
The Writings of Louie
The Complete Saga

Short Stories

Perchance to Dream

Praise for Perchance to Dream

A Fantasy both logical and compelling—a true otherself experience.

Jim Bennett
Poet and Amazon Reviewer

Website for Jon P. Gunn

ONE

THE SAINT AND THE TURTLE

The Saint, the Turtle, and a massive boulder first met in the treacherous pass through the heights of the Spina Mundi, a region infested with rocs, griffins, and wolves and customarily avoided by travelers unless they were in a great hurry. This particular pass was the shortest route between the upland provinces and the plain, and those who made it through alive could save as much as a week of travel.

The boulder had toppled from a precipice and was hurtling earthward, accelerating at thirty-two feet per second squared. The Saint, stereotypically garbed in the brown, hooded robe of a certified holy man, was walking serenely along the trail below, his hands tucked in his loose sleeves, his mind on uplifting thoughts. The Turtle, a brawny young man in the neo-Roman armor of the period and a gold-plated helmet which identified him as a general officer in the Imperial Regular Army, rounded a bend at that precise moment, appraised the remarkable scene, and futilely bellowed a warning.

He watched in sick horror as the boulder struck. The ground quaked violently, thunderous echoes crashed through the gorge, and the grisly spectacle was cloaked by a billowing pall of dust, through which smaller rocks and gravel continued to fall for some time.

Like any professional soldier, the Turtle could be counted on for prompt, level-headed action in an emergency. Dropping his luggage by the trail and ignoring the hail of pebbles that rattled off his helmet, cuirass, and epaulettes, he charged into the choking dust. First aid was presumably out of the question, but perhaps he could remove the mangled remains to a suitable place for burial.

Arriving at the site of the accident, he discovered the boulder was of unwieldy size. The Turtle knew he could not lift more than 925 pounds, and that only in the convenient form of a gymnasium bar-bell, while this rock weighed several tons. He made a quick circuit of it. Finding no limbs protruding from underneath, he concluded sadly that it had scored a direct hit, compressing its victim like a concertina. The body would have to be picked up with a sponge, if at all.

Still, he could not abandon a fellow man without first doing everything possible. He found solid footing for his iron-cleated military sandals, got a grip on the boulder, clenched his teeth, and gave a mighty heave. His classic features contorted with exertion. Ox-like muscles, developed over many years of calisthenics and clean living, rippled and bunched. Despite his best effort, the boulder moved only a fraction of an inch and settled back in place when he released it.

The Turtle stood back, doffed his golden helmet, and mopped his brow with the back of a powerful forearm. For a job like this, one needed chains, hooks, pulleys, and a team of Percherons. The Turtle set his helmet on the ground, put his right hand on his chin and his left hand on his right elbow, and analytically reappraised the task. Direct application of manpower had failed, but it might still be feasible to move the boulder with a lever. He looked around for something suitable, such as a resilient sapling, but there was nothing in view. The fact was, no sapling had grown anywhere in the Spina Mundi since the creation of the world; nor, for that matter, had a bush, or a flower, or a leaf of grass, or any of the creatures that lived on these things. The region was completely lifeless except for an abundance of dangerous carnivores, subsisting on each other, and when fortune favored, on human wayfarers.

The Turtle turned back to the boulder and reluctantly drew his sword. He would not have hesitated to use the weapon as a crowbar if he had thought there was any chance of saving a life, but in this case, it was a mere gesture, and good Damascus steel was hard to come by in those days.

"Salve," greeted the Saint, materializing through the dust.

The Turtle looked up. "You're alive," he exclaimed, sheathing his sword. "You gave me quite a turn—I could have sworn you were under this rock." He picked up his helmet and dusted it off with his handkerchief, for soldiers are always careful about their appearance. However, the Turtle's armor bore the nicks and dents of many a warlike encounter. One could see that he burnished it every day. The three vertical military creases in his red mantle were precisely parallel.

"You were deceived by sensory impressions, my son," said the Saint. "The boulder actually landed several cubits behind me." He spoke slowly, articulating each syllable with care. His voice was gentle, restful, and well-modulated, like background music.

There was a fresh shower of rocks from overhead; the boulder had been only a harbinger of greater things. The Turtle looked up in alarm. "I'm glad you're safe," he said, "but may I suggest we move on, quickly? The avalanche is going to start again any second."

"The danger," said the Saint, "is only apparent—another sensory illusion. Neither of us is destined to die today."

The Turtle looked at him blankly for several seconds before he replied, for he was a born leader of men. Being contradicted always took him completely by surprise. The Saint's eyes, he noticed, were large, luminously brown, and kindly. Behind the customary flowing white beard, his countenance reflected the deep inner tranquility to which all saints professionally aspired. It was impossible to question his judgment.

"I suppose those cliffs are really more solid than they look," the Turtle admitted, glancing up at the jagged blocks of granite piled vertically against the cliff. As he spoke, he distinctly saw movement among the boulders, and more pebbles fell. He also noted a pair of vultures, circling alertly at low altitude.

"I shall wait while you pick up your luggage," said the Saint.

"My luggage?" said the Turtle absently. "Oh, of course." He was determined not to appear nervous, even with good reason, for he was a warrior through and through, and he attached great importance to raw courage for its own sake. Staunchly suppressing his own good sense, he walked back to retrieve his duffle bag. He heaved it to his shoulder and rejoined the Saint.

They set out down the canyon and had scarcely reached the safety of the next bend when there was a tremendous roar from behind them, and the ground shook like a drenched cur. The Turtle wheeled to face the new threat, reaching instinctively for his sword.

"What's that?" he shouted, his voice barely audible above the noise.

The Saint waited until the landslide had spent its force and left relative quiet before he tried to answer. "It is just the avalanche that you predicted," he said placidly. "There is no cause for alarm."

The Turtle sheathed his sword again, feeling rather foolish, and caught up with the Saint. He tried to compose himself, or, alternatively, to convince himself that even a brave man was justified in being wary of loud noises in country known to be dangerous. As they went on, he looked up frequently at the cliffs on either side of the path, telling himself he was just watching for wild animals. Actually, the poised boulders had developed a compelling fascination in the last ten minutes. So had the vultures, of which there were now half a dozen.

"I have to admire your aplomb," he told the Saint, "It's too bad men with nerves like yours don't join the army—although I suppose the Church needs good men, too. That was a close call you had with that boulder."

"Not at all," the Saint replied. "I deliberately quickened my pace, to be ahead of the spot where the boulder was destined to strike."

"Then you did know it was coming?"

"I am a saint, my son."

"I see. Perhaps you can set me straight on a point: it was my understanding that saintly faculties applied only to human affairs. Aren't matters of pure geology a little outside the Church's baili-wick, on this world?"

"Normally they are, but not in this instance, for the boulder and the subsequent avalanche directly affected two human beings. It is impossible to draw so fine a distinction between the human and the non-human affairs of the world, for there is no real difference from a cosmic point of view. Also, you must bear in mind that the Omniscience of the Universe is, by definition, infinite knowledge, so that revealed knowledge, though it be only the minutest fraction of Omniscience, must still be virtually unlimited, and certainly must go beyond the scope of mere human affairs."

"Hmm," said the Turtle, "looking at it mathematically. I think I see...yes...any fraction of infinity..."

"It is not a simple concept," the Saint added, "unless one is enlightened."

"Nevertheless, the mathematical analogy is good, even if it's only an analogy. Of course, fractional Omniscience would be nonsense, considered in those terms. I think I'll make a note of that if you don't mind stopping for half a minute."

"It is only a quotation from the Scripture," said the Saint, but he obligingly stopped. At the same time, the soldier set down his duffle bag, took a stylus and tabella out of his helmet (He kept his razor and toothbrush there too; there were no pockets in a military kilt), and made a memorandum.

"Well, father," said the Turtle when they were on their way again, "here we are knee-deep in the Universe's mysteries, and still total strangers. Shall we introduce ourselves?"

"There is no need. My name and background are of no importance whatever; and the Supreme Commander of the Imperial Regular Army would hardly need an introduction, even if I were not gifted with direct perception."

"As you prefer," said the Turtle, shrugging the shoulder that was not supporting the duffle bag, "but please amend that title.

I'm 'Supreme Commander, Retired,' I resigned my commission some time ago."

"The title I used was not an error," said the Saint. "I am allowed to inform you that you are destined to regain your former command."

"Oh? That's encouraging. Would I be out of bounds if I asked you how soon?"

"The day after tomorrow. Your re-enlistment and simultaneous promotion are fully in accord with Destiny's Plan."

"Destiny?" said the Turtle, vaguely apprehensive. "Does that concern me?"

"Destiny concerns everyone, my son."

"Well. I suppose in the broader sense. I intend to do all I can to help preserve moral government, in its hour of greatest peril, but I hadn't thought of it as Destiny, exactly."

"Nearly all activity in the real universe is part of Destiny's Plan," murmured the Saint dreamily, "for Destiny is the manifest will of All There Is. Anomalies do occur, but your return to the Empire's service is not one of them. It has been predestined from the beginning of time."

"I suppose so," said the Turtle cautiously. He was quite well-read in many fields, but theology was one subject that had always baffled him. Based as it was on absolute rather than empirical fact, it confused most people.

"You will be well received by his Imperial Radiance," the Saint added.

"The Emperor?" said the Turtle in surprise. "Hardly. Crossing with the Emperor again would be the worst thing I could do."

The Saint sighed. Until that morning, when he had left the monastery to plunge once more into the seething world of unillumined laity, he had scarcely interrupted his secluded meditation for twenty years. Inevitably, he had almost forgotten how difficult it was to explain things to anyone but another saint.

"My son," he said patiently, "to suggest that what is destined is in any way wrong or undesirable is a contradiction of terms, by any but the pettiest human standards. A man of your intellect should never allow himself such cloudy thinking."

"I'd never presume to hazard a value-judgment in the presence of a saint," protested the Turtle, "but the plain fact is, the Emperor and I don't get along. He and I have had several disagreements, some of them political, and if my re-enlistment comes to his attention. I may even be denied the opportunity to serve at a time when the army needs every experienced officer it can get. That would be quite an annoyance. I might add, after having walked all this distance."

He frowned at this recollection. The Turtle spent his time between enlistments at his grandfather's farm. A few days earlier, his impulsive decision to drop everything and resume his military career had resulted in a heated argument over who had greater need for their only horse. The old farmer had firmly closed his mind to reason, and the Turtle had been obliged to set out on foot for the Capital. Although an infantry officer loves nothing better than a brisk hike across three provinces, carrying at least his own weight in armor and personal effects, the horse would have saved him valuable time.

"Please bear in mind," said the Saint apologetically, "that shaving your beard and enlisting under an assumed name is not entirely honest."

The Turtle's frown deepened. He had confided this plan to no one. He had never met any saints personally before and had not realized how disconcerting their company could be. "As a matter of fact," he replied archly, "I've given it a great deal of meticulous thought. I detest falsity in every form, and I'd never have settled on my present plans if I were not convinced that my duty as a soldier comes first."

"A choice between two evils," said the Saint sadly, "is often only apparent. Please forgive my speaking frankly, but it is so in this case, for by approaching the Emperor directly, you need compromise neither your scruples nor your sense of duty."

"Oh, needn't I? And suppose the Emperor won't listen—as he might not, having expressly forbidden me ever to show my face within twenty leagues of the Capital. Suppose I can't get an audience in the first place; emperors are busy men, you know, even in the best of times—and these are hardly the best of times. The barbarians are about to violate our northern frontiers, the commoners in every province are on the verge of revolt, and the nobility is impotently tied up in litigation over the imperial legacy. Never before in history has civilization been threatened from so many quarters at once. The Empire depends on the Imperial Regular Army, and I have to get back to it in time. How do you think I'll feel if I end up still a civilian, helplessly watching the Empire overrun by barbarians?" It was a numbing thought. "I'd rather join the army as a spearman E-1," he added.

The Saint closed his eyes and looked grieved. "You are destined to make a favorable impression on the Emperor," he murmured," Please do not allow a fine mind like yours to be misled by logical inference."

"Destined?" mumbled the Turtle, suddenly remembering why one does not argue with a saint. "Oh. I see; I must have misunderstood you."

The Saint acknowledged this apology with a kindly smile and

relapsed into meditative silence. The Turtle examined the shattered fragments of his plan and wondered how it had ever come to his mind. Now that he thought about it, it was not only dishonest but actually rather cowardly. Yes, the Saint was right. What other good way was there for a man of the Turtle's temperament to manage his affairs? All his greatest deeds had been accomplished by charging into the thick of things. He had won several famous military victories just that way, sometimes single-handedly.

There would be difficulties, of course. First, he had to get an audience with the Emperor, and the Emperor had little time these days to hear his subjects' petitions. The only place to meet him face to face would be in the nearly-inviolable Imperial Hall of Kings. Once inside, he would have to state his case quickly before he was thrown out again.

Nevertheless, it could be done. The Hall was always in emergency session, of late, but the presence of forty-one provincial delegates and all their functionaries would be more an asset than a hindrance. A dominant personality like the Turtle was always most successful when dealing with crowds of people. In private personal contacts, there were occasional individuals—like the Turtle's grandfather, or like the Emperor—who were too bigoted to be moved by any array of logic, but the chance that such people would comprise the majority of a group was negligibly slim. This applied to all groups, without exception. In theory, and usually in practice, it was equally simple to get full cooperation from a company of rebellious recruits, a crowd of unruly civilians, a band of robbers, or a plenary session of the Imperial Hall of Kings. It was just a matter of knowing what to say and how to say it. It would take a man with the Turtle's abilities to join the army as Supreme Commander, but it could be done.

The Turtle wanted to ask whether it would be worth the effort and risk—whether there was really much hope of saving the disintegrating Empire—but he hesitated. Holy men were not mere astrologers, to be consulted on any little question. Their spiritual insight gave them awesome powers, which they were absolutely forbidden to abuse.

The Saint and the Turtle walked on for several hours, mostly in silence. The Saint's mind was on spiritual matters, which are not easily put into words, and should not ordinarily be discussed with the laity anyway. The Turtle dropped remarks from time to time, but although the Saint always listened politely, his replies were pious monosyllables, which left no room for further comment.

Finally, they emerged from the canyon and came to a fork in the road. They paused of one accord, and the Turtle set down his duffle bag to rest his shoulder.

"We part here," said the Saint, "for my road lies south, to Kalopolis. There is one more thing I must tell you before we go our separate ways."

"Yes?" said the Turtle, preparing to hear something of deep moral significance.

"If you have occasion to change any resolve or opinion, you must wait for either for the Summer or the Winter Solstice. You must never change your mind at any other time of year."

It took the Turtle a few moments to absorb this, then he laughed heartily. "That," he said, "is the wisest counsel I've ever heard, and I'll follow it to the letter. Please be assured that I've never changed my mind in my life."

"Very seldom," the Saint agreed, "and then only in adaptation to changing circumstances. I know your character, my son, and I know that your powers of resolve will carry you through many difficulties wherein a weaker man would falter, but—" He spread his hands in a gesture of apology. "—these are dangerous, historically pivotal times, and the ways of Destiny are not always fathomable to the lay mind. Only by strict adherence to this rule can you be sure to avoid temptation."

"Very well, father," said the warrior agreeably, "but what's so auspicious about the solstices?"

"The Universe has decreed them so in your case. It is beyond my power adequately to explain to the unenlightened, but you must have faith in the wisdom of the Cosmos. If you do not, you may cause dangerous anomalies in the Plan of Destiny and put the priesthood of the Established Faith to a great deal of trouble."

"You have my solemn promise," said the Turtle, but really it's superfluous. I can't imagine why I'd ever want to change my mind. It just isn't my nature."

"So much the better if you never do," said the Saint kindly, "but please be on your guard. Farewell, my son and the blessings of All There Is be with you. We shall meet again, before long."

The Turtle stood and watched the Saint until he was out of sight, puzzling over the ominous parting words, and, for that matter, over the whole afternoon's conversation. Theological matters, by their very nature, could be quite distressing to the orderly and incisive mind of a trained soldier.

The Turtle shrugged, took out his tablet and stylus, and made a note of the oracle. Then he shouldered his duffle bag and strode on his way, marching, as always, to the pulse of imaginary snare-drums.

TWO
AZAZA

Azaza, a young woman of many talents, few scruples, and unbelievable beauty, lived quietly in the Capital city, in a small but richly-furnished house a few doors up the street from the Teahouse of the Three Moons. She plied her disreputable trade, avoided politics and publicity, and bothered no one but her clients.

At that time, living quietly in the Capital was something of an accomplishment, for this was the natural geopolitical focus of several distinct and conflicting tides of history. Riots and demonstrations were a daily occurrence. Wherever one looked, the walls were defaced with antifeudalist slogans. Military police nervously patrolled the city in pairs or groups, dodging stones, bottles, and rotten vegetables. Spies were everywhere that year. They skulked in every alley, lined up three abreast behind every door, and queued up at strategic keyholes.

Nor was staying out of politics as easy as it sounds, for subversion was rampant. Four out of five citizens were at least part-time activists for some faction or other. Subversive organizations were cropping up faster than the police could catalogue them, let alone suppress them. These groups were as diverse as they were numerous. There was a cause for every human temperament and one or more organizations for every cause. They all agreed the feudal system had outlived its historical usefulness and should now be replaced, as violently and dramatically as possible, with something newer, but their disunity in all other regards made negotiation impossible. If there had been just one huge revolutionary party, the Conservatives could have tried to appease it. As it was, a concession to one faction would have been considered the last straw by all the others, and if even one decided it was time to revolt, all the others would have to join in or risk missing their golden opportunity.

Not all the factions were composed of commoners. Even the nobles were divided, though not over ideology. The reigning Emperor was stricken in years and had neither direct heir nor next of kin. Pretenders to the succession had cropped up in every province, backing their claims with spurious documents and enormous feudal armies. Litigation was proceeding in an orderly fashion through the Supreme Tribunal, so far, but all the pretenders had promised to resort to arms if the Tribunal's final decision fell short of perfect fairness. Here, again, if the Emperor had decided in favor of one king, it would have meant secession by the other forty.

Not all the factions were even subversive. The Turtle himself had founded one, some months before, upon resigning his command in a fit of pique. It was a wholeheartedly loyal and patriotic organization, little more than a Committee for Unsolicited Advice to the Government. Its members styled themselves Dynamic Feudalists, and their sole deviation from hidebound right-thinking was to advocate aristocratic titles for high-ranking officers of the Imperial Regular Army who had distinguished themselves in the Empire's service. The membership consisted solely of high-ranking officers of the Imperial Regular Army who had distinguished themselves in the Empire's service.

Azaza, however, was a neutral—not a member of the organized Neutral Party, which was covertly raising an army of its own and was no more neutral than the Radicals—but a genuine neutral. She remained carefully uninvolved and uncommitted, smoothly changing the subject whenever politics was mentioned.

For the most part, Azaza was typical of the youth of her generation—materialistic, libertine, shallow, irreligious, and pseudo-intellectual—but in certain ways, she was distinctly atypical. In craft and avarice, she surpassed the shrewdest of the Neutrals, and few Radicals could have matched her in moral flippancy. Most importantly, in stark physical beauty, she outshone the noblest-born of the Conservatives' ladies by thousands of lush, sultry candlepower. The perfection of her features had set new, unattainable standards for art students, and she had a figure upon which nature had bestowed every possible grace so deftly, yet in such lavish abundance, that even usurers, judges, morticians, tax agents and the like would stop to gaze in near-human astonishment when she passed by.

Azaza's mother had been a professional sorceress, and her father evidently an incubus. Girls did not attend public schools in those days, and the education Azaza received from her mother was poorly rounded. She learned to apply the evil eye when she was only six, after which the other children in her neighborhood avoided her. During her most formative years, her only playmates were those she learned to call up from the nether worlds; her only social life, the Witches' Sabbath; and her only recreation moonlight rides on an enchanted airborne goat. She grew up feeling left out, unloved, different, and for some mystical reason, this took the form of an obsessive ambition to become Empress of the realm. In a way, Azaza was a subversive party all by herself.

At the age of fourteen, she had grown tired of the apprenticeship, so she had cast a spell on her mother and left home. Fending for herself had turned out to be ridiculously easy. Bad upbringing and overpowering beauty had determined her profession almost before she knew it.

Azaza was in her boudoir, admiring herself in a hand mirror when the bell sounded at the front gate. This was followed, after a short delay, by sounds of harsher and harsher quarreling, the words of which were garbled by their own profusion and muffled by the rich foliage of the courtyard garden. Azaza's housemaid rushed into the room.

"It's the Scarecrow again," the girl announced. "The gateman tried to put him off, but you know how he is. He tried to tell us you were expecting him."

Azaza yawned sensuously. "The Scarecrow," she said, "is becoming a nuisance. Tell him he's having hallucinations again— my only appointment this afternoon is with the Leader of the Neutral Party."

"Ha! You know how much good that'll do! The Scarecrow

hates Neutrals with a passion, besides being the jealous type. He'll wait around for the Leader, and then you'll really see what bad publicity's made of."

Azaza reluctantly set down her mirror, rose from her couch, strolled languidly to the front window, and peered out through the lattice.

"He does look purposeful," she admitted.

The unappreciated caller outside the wrought-iron gate was of a little less than medium height, very thin, and rumpled. He wore a tattered scholar's robe, which was too big for him. He had a pinched, fanatic face, mad, brooding eyes, and soot-colored hair that had never been combed. He was shaking the bars of the gate as he waited for the maid to return.

Azaza turned away from the lattice with a thoughtful moue.

"You could have him arrested," said the maid. "I don't know why you keep putting it off."

Azaza did not know either, except for an occasional spark of self-suspicion, which she always hastily stamped out before it became a conscious thought. "Because he owes me four hundred crowns," she rationalized impatiently.

"In jail or out, he'll never be able to pay it."

"Don't be too sure. He's an alchemist—quite a competent one; he used to have a professorship at the Imperial Institute of Natural Philosophy, till he was fired for refusing to sign a loyalty oath. Alchemists make gold, and the Scarecrow's working on a process of his own. Once it's perfected, he can make four hundred crowns out of its weight in scrap iron, but he can't experiment if he's in jail."

"That's silly," said the maid. "If you don't charge him with anything worse than loitering, he'll only be in jail overnight."

"It's not silly," Azaza returned. "He belongs to some Radical organization, and the police suspect him.

If they have some excuse to arrest him, they'll grill him till he loses his temper and blurts out enough to convict himself; and then I'll never see my money. Besides, why get him in that much trouble? I have nothing against him—it's just that he doesn't pay his bills."

"I think he's a demoralizing influence on other clients—that do pay their bills."

Azaza sighed. "Yes, he's a nuisance. Compromise, then.

Threaten him. Tell him I won't see him till he pays what he owes me, and if he won't leave me alone, I'll complain to the police."

"I hope he takes the hint," said the maid, and went to relay the message. Through her lattice, Azaza watched the maid tell the gateman, and the gateman tell the Scarecrow. The maid fled into the house, and the gateman took cover in his gatehouse as the scientist shouted abuses, shook his fists, threw cobblestones, and rattled the heavy iron grating. He did give up and leave somewhat sooner than usual.

Although she would never admit it, Azaza was more depressed than irritated by these incidents. Sometime before, when she had priced herself into the higher social strata, leaving her less affluent admirers to pine away, or take to drink and opium, or join the frontier legions, or enter monasteries, the Scarecrow had refused to be weeded out. He had fumed and ranted, demanded credit, threatened Azaza with violence, and on one occasion had tried to drive his rivals from her house with a horsewhip. It was too bad, Azaza thought, that so few of her admirers had the Scarecrow's ability to translate affection into overt ferocity. The world was too full of self-conscious fumblers and apologetic, moon-gazing esthetes, and a lunatic like the Scarecrow could be a refreshing change of pace.

However, there were more important things in life. Theodora, chief among Azaza's idols, had not won her place in history by wasting time and talent on a penniless alchemist.

THREE

THE SAINT AND THE PATRIARCH

The Saint arrived in Kalopolis and proceeded with neither haste nor delay on his first errand. This was his natal town, and if he had been an ordinary layman, he might have been tempted to spend an hour or so wandering through the poignantly familiar streets, steeping himself in memories. He was a saint, however, and had too broad a perspective to be distracted by anything as temporal as his birthplace.

He had come to see his former teacher, the Patriarch of Kalopolis. The Patriarch's gateman admitted the Saint to the courtyard and went to announce him. While he waited, the Saint looked around the garden. It had changed, as all things must, since he had last seen it. The vines were thicker. Part of the rock garden had been replaced with shrubbery. An old shade tree had died, and a sapling was growing in its place. The most conspicuous change was the addition of a marble statue, depicting a bevy of nymphs dancing nudely in the middle of the fountain. A fleeting look of sorrow and pity crossed the Saint's face. His old teacher had not changed.

In a few minutes, the aged Patriarch himself hobbled from the house and welcomed the Saint with open arms.

"Salve, boy, salve!" he cackled." Welcome back to civilization, or what passes for civilization in these heretical times. I swear it's been twenty years if it's been a day! But why stand around out here? Why didn't you come right in? You should know by now how much stock I take in punctilio among old friends. Come on in out of the sun!"

The Patriarch was eighty-nine years old, thin as a hoarse whisper and senile as a pterodactyl, which he also resembled physically in some respects—there was something decidedly reptilian about him, especially the dry, scaly complexion. All the color in his wizened face was concentrated in his nose, which was a startling cherry-red. He wore a black ecclesiastical robe and a skullcap.

The Saint followed the Patriarch into the library, a quietly tasteful room at first glance until one happened to notice that the pictures on the walls were frankly lascivious, or until one browsed through the books which lined three sides of the room, and discovered that the pornography outnumbered the religious works by about three volumes to two. On top of one bookcase, posing as *objets d'art*, stood a row of ivory carvings of lewd heathen goddesses.

"Twenty years," repeated the Patriarch unbelievingly. "How did you maintain your sanity? I assume you achieved enlightenment during those twenty years? Of course, or you wouldn't have come back till you did, would you? But surely you haven't been just working on enlightenment, all this time."

"No, father," said the Saint.

"Then they just kept you waiting around for a mission worthy of your talents, didn't they? Stockpiled, I call it. That does sometimes happen when a saint turns out to have uncommon ability, and I always knew you had. Twenty years, though! It's a good thing the Universe finally thought of something for you to do. So, what will you do in this illusory world of human beings, now that you're back?"

"Whatever is destined, father," replied the Saint.

The Patriarch broke into a raucous cackle of amusement. "Spoken like a true saint!" he cheered. "I couldn't have answered that question more piously myself! Spoken like a saint among saints! Sit down, boy; rest your feet; make yourself at home. Here, now, what can I offer you to drink?" He drew a sliding panel aside and indicated the well-stocked liquor cabinet with a sweep of his thin hand.

"A little water, if you please," said the Saint.

"Water! Come now, my boy; your trials are supposed to be past! There's no more need to abstain from the good things. How many times have you heard me say the proscription of alcohol is an outmoded superstition?"

"Only water, thank you," the Saint insisted gently.

The Patriarch looked hurt. "My son," he said gravely, laying one hand on the Saint's shoulder, "all the years you studied under me, at the Seminary and then as a private student, I was always meticulously careful to distinguish between the real essence of the Singlefold Path and the superficial canonical garbage of the Established Faith. Pious austerities are useful, in their way, as elementary exercises, but they have nothing whatever to do with genuine saintliness. Is it possible, after all my careful tutoring, that you've so completely missed the point? If this is some tripe they've been feeding you at the monastery, the abbot's going to hear plenty from me!"

"I have been away for twenty years, father," said the Saint. "It is not my spirit, but my corporeal being, which I must acclimate gradually to the ways of human beings."

The Patriarch gave his disciple a deeply searching—and not unsuspicious—look, then abandoned the argument with a shrug. "Well, everyone to his own good taste," he said tolerantly. He sat down and helped himself to a shot of absinthe from the flagon by his couch. "Though I never knew you to turn down a snort before," he added. "You played your hottest music when you were about half staggered, as I recall."

He struck a small gong, and a serving girl appeared instantly, as if from nowhere.

"Water for my honored guest," ordered the Patriarch.

"Draw it fresh from the well."

The girl vanished.

"Best water in Kalopolis comes from my well," the old man said, "if you happen to like water. That girl is Melli, my chief cook and bottle opener. The name's short for Mellisuga-helenae. I called her that for her small size and great speed, but the full name's a bit pompous for a girl of sixteen, don't you think?"

Melli returned almost immediately with a pitcher of water.

"Fastest girl in Kalopolis," the Patriarch explained proudly. The girl was small and gracefully slender and very pretty in a demure and retiring way, as though she realized that no one who worked for a patriarch had any right to be attractive, and she was very sorry, but she could not help it. The Patriarch leered at her openly, but she pretended not to notice. She poured the Saint a tumbler of water. He thanked her without looking at her, and she disappeared again.

"Well, my boy," said the Patriarch, "Lots of things have changed while you've been away. Your family. I'm sad to say...well..."

"A saint is free from worldly attachments," said the Saint.

"I guess I won't have to fill you in on the past twenty years, will I?"

"No, father."

"Of course not, now that you're a saint. I'm glad I don't have to break the news—though I guess not even a layman would be much surprised, after being gone twenty years. One by one, all your relatives have joined the Great Majority. Your two tame sparrows were the first to go. Your sister was the last. Tragic accident."

"It was destined," said the Saint.

"They all got the finest funerals I could arrange," the Patriarch consoled. "I personally said the last rites for each of them—even the birds."

"I am grateful for your kindness," said the Saint. "Think nothing of it. It was the least I could do for the family of my most promising disciple. Ah, well; I suppose we could find a more cheerful subject. Let's enjoy the fruits of life while they're in season, I always say, and refrain from mumbling yesterday's pits. I've saved your guitar carefully for your return. Keeping it waxed and polished for you has been one of Melli's regular chores. Melli?"

She appeared in a flash.

"Fetch the guitar, will you?"

The Patriarch tried to pinch her as she passed his couch, but he was much too slow. Melli crossed the room, opened an ornate Chinese cabinet, took the instrument out, and brought it to the Saint, all in about three seconds.

"Thank you," said the Saint, but Melli was already gone.

"She's bashful around strangers," said the Patriarch. "Fast but bashful, heh heh. Some people find her speed disconcerting, but you get used to it after a while. She's the most efficient housekeeper in Kalopolis. She can do a week's marketing in four minutes flat—I clocked her once. Well, boy, play us a tune. It's been a mighty long time."

The Saint, looking introspective, resettled the guitar on his knees. The guitar was of a foreign style, with thirteen steel strings. The usual six were backed by a fretted fingerboard, while the seven heavier strings were alongside the neck, giving the instrument a harp-like appearance that accented the Saint's demeanor. It was fashioned of some dark, exotic wood, rich in hue, burnished to a glassy finish, and elaborately ornamented with silver tracery and pearl inlays. The neck terminated in a carved dog's head and bristled with tuning pegs.

The Saint thoughtfully fretted a string with his left forefinger.

"The neck hasn't warped a bit in twenty years," said the Patriarch. "That thing's had the best of care if I do say so myself. I've even seen that it was kept in new strings. I'll bet it's in tune, right now."

"Again, I am very grateful," said the Saint. He fingered a chord and poised the plectrum over the strings but did not strike them. After a moment of suspense, he set the guitar aside.

"I am too badly out of practice," he apologized.

The Patriarch was visibly disappointed, but one does not try to coax a saint. He drank his absinthe and changed the subject again, "So you'll do whatever's destined, will you? You've kept us in the dark long enough. I think, even for a saint. Maybe because I talk too much? Forgive an old man's prolixity, my boy; it's my reaction to fifty years of association with fellow saints, who don't do much talking, as well, you know. So what's it destined that you'll do, now that you're finally one with the Cosmos?"

The Saint tactfully refrained from reminding his teacher that he, too, could know everything if he would sober up for a while. "The task assigned me is to save the civilized world from the coming disaster," he said.

The Patriarch snorted contemptuously, "You too? Everybody talks about disaster these days, but nobody does anything. What if the masses do want to overthrow the government? The masses never know what's good for them—and neither does the government, for that matter. Besides, they're all cutting each other's throats for first crack at the big revolt. What faction's powerful enough to be a real threat? No. I've seen too much of this stuff in my day to work up much fever about it anymore. We saints aren't supposed to worry about politics anyway, you know."

"The fall of the Empire is destined, father, as is the destruction of the Established Faith."

The goblet stopped halfway to the Patriarch's withered lips. His eyes widened, and he turned deathly pale. "Destined...did I hear you right? The Church...?"

"Yes, father."

"How long's all this been going on?"

"It has been predestined since—"

"I know—since the beginning of time—but how long's the Church known about it?"

"It was revealed to His Saintliness five days ago, father, and has been official doctrine since the day before yesterday."

"Why doesn't the Prime Ecclesiarch keep me informed on developments like this?" the Patriarch complained. "He could have saved me having to rewrite a whole sermon, blast that overfed...but wait!" A light of understanding flickered in the Patriarch's dull eyes. "You said you could prevent this?"

"No, father; it is destined."

"Now, hold on! You just said you were going to save the civilized world from disaster."

"By disaster, father," the Saint explained patiently, "I meant a course of events other than that mapped out by Destiny for the Highest Good of the Universe. My mission is only to prevent profane hands from interfering with the plan."

"In other words, you've come to destroy the Empire and the Church!" the Patriarch accused. "Why mince words?"

"Not I, father. This Cataclysm is part of the plan."

"But that's preposterous! Why would the Universe want to destroy Its Church, the first Church in history to teach nothing but the Truth?"

The Saint smiled sadly and spread his hands.

The Patriarch tossed off his drink and poured another one, spilling some. "And what about all the people who depend on the Church for spiritual sustenance? What are they supposed to do—take up heathenism?"

The Saint nodded mutely.

"Confound it, boy," blurted the Patriarch, "if you destroy the Church, what will I do for a living? Do you think it's easy for a man my age to learn a new profession?"

"Destiny will provide for all things," the Saint soothed.

"So I notice," said the Patriarch dryly, "all in one fell swoop."

The Patriarch stared numbly into space, through the ensuing lull, periodically taking a gulp of absinthe. The Saint looked down at his clasped hands.

"Well," sighed the Patriarch at last, "I guess you're not to blame. We don't choose our destined missions in life to suit ourselves, do we?"

"No, father," said the Saint.

"Such is the way of the Universe," the old priest continued mournfully. "It moves, heeding not the fates of Its creatures. It's depressing, from a human point of view, that the only realistic religion there's ever been has to be dedicated to a Power Which has no purposes compatible with ours; of course, we saints have no business adopting a human point of view."

"No, father," the Saint agreed.

The Patriarch rose stiffly and shuffled to a bookcase, where he stood looking pensively at the three hundred forty-five volumes of Scripture. "You know," he said, "maybe I'm getting tender-minded, but sometimes I wonder if the old heathen cults didn't have something to teach us after all. I don't mean in the way of doctrines—our doctrines are true to the last apostrophe, and you can't ask for much more than that—I mean something else, outside the doctrines—a vital force—a life of their own, almost. The heathens had something we don't have, and I'm not convinced it was necessarily bad."

"All that was true or good in the heathen religions was incorporated into ours, father," said the Saint.

"I realize that; I'm talking about something else.

The higher critics have purged all the irrelevant pagan elements from our present, perfected doctrines, leaving nothing but the Truth, but how can we be sure they haven't accidentally thrown out something valuable along with the dross? Couldn't there be something outside the Truth—or beyond the Truth—or maybe in between it somewhere—that our early prophets overlooked? How else can you account for the Church's reaction now? When the heathen cults found themselves dying out in competition with our superior doctrines, they fought tooth and nail—they called us names, they split theological hairs, they condemned scientific progress, they even told lies from the pulpit! Then look at us: The Established Faith is to be destroyed—just like that. No questions. We saints are supposed to accept the Will of Destiny as the Highest Ultimate Good, but isn't this going too far? Does Destiny expect us to take this lying down?"

"Yes, father," said the Saint.

"Look here," cried the Patriarch, waving his hand angrily at the several shelves of Scripture. "Three hundred and forty-five volumes of raw Truth and every jot of it will stand up to the most ruthless logical and scientific scrutiny. It's a work of all-inclusive perfection. No fact of any validity can possibly lie outside its compass. Our doctrines contain all the Truth and nothing untrue. Are you telling me Destiny wants all this swept away?"

"No mortal can fathom the Will of Destiny, father."

"Right! That's my point! Nobody can fathom Destiny, not even a saint! Why not, pray tell? Our saints and prophets spent five hundred years compiling this thing; after that, every new revelation turned out to be a reiteration of what was already in the Scripture. That was seven hundred years ago. Now for seven centuries, we've had a perfect Scripture. We know all there is to know about religion, yet we still can't understand the Universe. Doesn't that tell you something?"

"We must not blame the Church, father, but rather the limitations of our finite mortal minds."

"All right, damn it! That means the Church is too good for us, and if it's too good for us, then it's not right for us! Modern science forced us to scrap all the pagan hogwash—salvation, immortality, the Golden Rule, divine intervention, and the rest of it—and revelation directed us to replace it all with sophisticated philosophical insight and resignation to Destiny. We're wondrous wise, now, but is wisdom really the comfort it's cracked up to be? The early prophets proved that immortal life would be a bore and a drag—proved it, mind you, *quod erat demonstrandum*, leaving no room for reasonable doubt—but is simple annihilation an adequate substitute? It makes sense, but is it the right kind of sense? What I mean is, why should a religion have to make sense in the first place? Science has to, and philosophy ought to, but I say religion should aim higher than that. We can extol annihilation as surcease from fleshly suffering, but have you ever tried to put it across to the faithful, like I have? The heathens never had that trouble; folks used to pack their churches every Sabbath! So we have the whole Truth now—so what? There's consolation in Truth for us saints because we have our spiritual insight and can adapt our wills to the Will of the Universe, but what good is it to the ordinary man-in-the-pew? What use is a religion that has nothing to offer but reams and reams of Truth? If I weren't the Patriarch of Kalopolis. I'd say it's a damned good thing this nightmare of clear theological thinking is about to be destroyed!"

The Saint continued to contemplate his folded hands, looking quietly grieved. The Patriarch sighed wearily, eased himself back to the cushions, and replenished his goblet.

"Forgive my getting carried away like that," he said. "I guess I lost my head for a minute. The Church has been my guidepost, as well as my bread-and-butter, for fifty years, and it comes as a terrible shock to learn that it's about to collapse. I should already have known, of course, but there it is again—I try to be human, as well as holy."

"Of course, father," replied the Saint gently.

"Do what is destined, my son. Go forth and save the Plan of a wanton Universe from the meddling of intelligent creatures, for that is your duty as a saint...er...how long will the Church last?"

"Seven months, father. It will be destroyed the day after the Winter Solstice."

"Then I can give your mission my blessing, which won't be completely meaningless for another seven months. I suppose your destiny will take you to the Capital?"

"Yes, father."

The Patriarch nodded knowingly. "Most destinies do, usually fairly early in the game. Be sure to call at the Temple of the Macrocosm, while you're there, and give my regards to the Prime Ecclesiarch."

"Yes, father," the Saint promised. "I shall, in fact, go to the Capital immediately. Most of my first errands are in that vicinity."

"I'll watch your progress with great interest, these next seven months," said the Patriarch. "What do your first errands consist of, there in the center of the Empire? You can tell me—I'm illumined too."

"As a matter of fact, father. I can tell you very little since I myself try to refrain from prying too deeply into the plan. Spiritual insight is not to be used idly."

"Don't lecture me, boy! Tell me whatever you can. I'll look the rest up in the Book of Prophesy."

"First, I must rescue a man with an important destiny, who will try to avoid it, through suicide."

"Fine; there's always a few of those, aren't there? What after that?"

"Next, I must counsel a young woman, whose personal destiny will need careful guidance."

"It takes all kinds to wreck an empire, doesn't it? Is she anyone I know'?"

"I should hope not, father."

The Patriarch gave a shrug of exaggerated indifference. "They're all alike to us saints, but they do have different names. As I said. I'd like to look this cataclysm up in the Scripture, and it's hard enough to find things in that jungle when you know what you're looking for."

The Saint stared down at the floor and replied almost in a whisper. "Her name, father, is Azaza."

The Patriarch's false nonchalance collapsed. His pale eyes widened in disbelief, then narrowed and began twinkling lecherously. He fought to control a wicked grin, then to stifle a snicker. Failing in both efforts, he erupted into a crackling gale of mirth, "Azaza!" he crowed, slapping his bony knee. "Haw! You, of all people—you, who could never look a woman in the eye without blushing to the toenails—counseling the one and only Azaza! Oh, this is fabulous!" He winked obscenely. "As soon as you get back to Kalopolis. I want you to call on me right away and—heh heh—tell me how she is."

The Saint gave his erstwhile teacher a look of deep compassion and smiled very faintly, "Yes, father," he said.

"That sounds like the kind of destiny I could really go for myself," snickered the Patriarch, "but I'm afraid it's a job for—ah— younger blood, eh?"

"So it is, father," said the Saint, significantly stroking his white beard.

"Go, then, my son," said the Patriarch, struggling to control his unseemly amusement, "and my blessing, for what it's still worth in these Last Days. I'll wait here for the Cataclysm and endeavor to soften the shock of the terrible foreknowledge you've imparted to me by drowning myself in—hmm—in meditation. Hee-haw!"

He cackled merrily at his own wit and poured himself another drink.

It was obviously time for the Saint to depart.

FOUR

THE TURTLE AND THE EMPEROR

A cloud of neurotic indecision wreathed the brains of the Empire like an undeserved halo. In the Imperial Hall of Kings, the central parliamentary body to which each monarch of the forty-one provinces sent a close relative as a delegate, there was some muted conversation but no debate. They were at the end of their once-vast resources. The undertow of history was against them, and everything they had tried to do had made things worse. The assembled royalty now felt that even a false thought would be enough to upset the precarious poise of Conservative power and send the Old Order crashing.

The Hall of Kings stood with all the other government buildings inside the Imperial Citadel, an ancient, sprawling fortress left over from the dawn of the Empire's history. It was in the middle of the Capital city, although it had been the city wall in ancient times. The architects who had laid it out a thousand years before had had no way of knowing where the trends toward urbanization and big government would lead. In ensuing centuries the city had spilled over its walls to flood the surrounding countryside. At the same time, it was gradually crowded out of its original confines by government buildings. Now the city was outside the wall, and the inside was taken up by the Imperial Palace, the Hall of Kings, princely accommodations for the forty-one permanent delegates and their retinues, the Central Arsenal, offices of the Imperial Tax Commission, the Treasury and its four annexes, the Supreme Tribunal and the Tower of Justice, the Public Archives (where the proceedings of the Hall of Kings were stored forever in triplicate), the Imperial Institute of Natural Philosophy (maintained by the government in case a brain trust was suddenly needed), and all the other institutions a civilized government needed to keep the affairs of forty-one provinces running smoothly.

This mighty citadel contained not only the whole Empire in distilled essence but a cross-section of the world at large, for space had been found for embassies and culture-centers of every major barbarian nation. In fact, the whole Universe was represented here, for the ancient Temple of the Macrocosm, cerebral ganglion of the Established Faith, had been inside the fortress since long before the fortress was built, and the subject of tearing it down to make room for another government building was never broached, by anyone, ever.

The Turtle's hike to the Capital took another day and a half after he left the Saint, and he arrived in an excellent frame of mind. He had a rosy premonition that everything was going to work out perfectly. He stopped at an inn just long enough to burnish his dusty armor, dash off an address to the Hall of Kings, and then proceed at once to the Imperial Citadel.

It was good to see those louring walls again. The unsightly gray ramparts, protectively coiled around the government, lent moral support to the whole feudal tradition and made the dire predictions of sage and fanatic alike very hard to take seriously. The sheer size of the fortress was impossible to describe except in colorless numbers, difficult even to imagine except in terms of one's own experience: The Turtle knew the Imperial Regulars had to keep several companies of recruits constantly on police detail, just to keep the interior free of litter.

These impenetrable walls would be an unmixed blessing when the revolt once started, but the Turtle knew the sense of security they inspired meanwhile was treacherous. Since most of the Empire was outside the walls, the walls alone could not keep revolt from breaking out.

Still, it was good to see them. It would be good, too, to get back to the army, where one's subordinates were men and not mules, and thus open to reason, and where a man could come to dinner in full armor, if he was so inclined, without being snickered at.

The Turtle crossed the most convenient of several drawbridges, passed through the open gate, and made his way through familiar streets to the Hall of Kings. There he met the day's first hurdle—the guards at the portals. They confronted him with drawn swords as he approached, and brusquely recited the standard, memorized, totally incontestable warning that they were under strict orders to admit no visitors while the Hall was in session.

The Turtle did not argue the point. He merely called the guards to attention and inspected them. He found a tiny nick in one man's sword, an improperly knotted thong on another's sandal, and two or three microscopic flecks of rust on another's left epaulette. He gave them a stern admonishment to try harder thenceforth and entered the building, congratulating himself for his understanding of men.

A few moments later, he strode impressively, though unannounced, into the assembly chamber itself. A surprised mutter arose at the irregular intrusion, then scattered laughter as the delegates recognized the Turtle without his beard.

"So you're back," said the Emperor sourly.

The Turtle approached the Round Table, carrying his helmet on his left arm, and saluted the assembly. "I have returned at this time," he confirmed, his great voice echoing from the domed ceiling, "for it is my conviction that in these perilous times, when—"

"With the same old complaints, no doubt," the Emperor suggested. There was snickering among the delegates.

"As a matter of fact," said the Turtle, "no."

The delegates broke into applause. The Turtle frowned. Things were not going nearly as smoothly as he had expected. The Secretary Royal gaveled briskly, and order was restored.

"We're glad this isn't going to be another re-run of previous arguments," said the Emperor.

"We presume you're aware that barging in here while the Hall is in session is a serious criminal offense—a political crime, in fact. This isn't the first time you've done it, but while you were still of some use, we chose to overlook many of your idiosyncrasies. This time, however—"

"Your Radiance. I—"

"Silence! Interrupting the Emperor is another offense you've committed much too often. By your actions today, you've condemned yourself to...what was it? It's been so long since the law's been enforced..."

"Ten to thirty years, your Radiance," the Secretary Royal supplied.

"Yes, you've condemned yourself to thirty years in the Tower of Justice. However, We're a fair-minded man. We're assuming you wouldn't have forfeited the best thirty years of your life this way unless you had something of utmost importance to say. Therefore, before you're thrown in irons, you may speak."

Pikemen of the Imperial Guard stepped into position behind the prisoner and on either flank.

"Thank you, your Radiance," said the Turtle doubtfully.

Seeing nothing to do but proceed according to plan, he extracted a sheaf of notes from his helmet. "Your Radiance," he began, "distinguished Majesties, and fellow citizens of the Empire: I have returned at this time to offer my services because it is my conviction that in these perilous times when the Empire—"

"And be brief," said the Emperor, correcting what he saw had been a serious oversight. The Turtle tucked the notes back inside his helmet. Fortunately, he had had the foresight to commit them to memory.

"I have returned at this time to offer my services," he averred, "because it is my conviction that in these perilous times, when the Empire is threatened by revolt from within, invasion from without, and an alarming decline in patriotic spirit among all the lower strata of society, the hour is at hand for all loyal citizens, nobles and commoners alike, to put aside their petty differences and rally to the defense of civilization, moral government, and our way of life. The foundation—the very substance—of Empire—"

"Hear, hear!" cried the delegates sportively.

"We appreciate your dedication," said the Emperor, "but you're a little late. Your former position has been filled. Or," he added sarcastically, "perhaps you were looking for something a little better?"

"No, your Radiance," said the Turtle; "all my training and experience have been in the field of military science, and although I'm overwhelmed by this unexpected offer of a post in the Imperial court—"

"Now who offered—?"

"—nevertheless, nevertheless," insisted the Turtle, "I feel that my greatest service to the Empire would be rendered in the field for which my background has best prepared me. May I add, if your Radiance and Majesties will permit me one word in my own recommendation, that never while I was Supreme Commander did a guard at the portals of the Imperial Hall of Kings report for duty with rusty armor or an improperly sharpened weapon... um...on my way in. I happened to notice these discrepancies, and some minor ones as well, among the sentries on duty at this very minute."

Silence followed this bombshell. The Emperor was visibly horrified, and the delegates were ashen. All nobles were well-schooled in military philosophy, and they were all fully aware of the advanced decay in morale and discipline revealed by these superficial signs. Seeing that he had captured his audience's sympathy with one deft stroke, the Turtle pressed on, quoting from his prepared address.

"The foundation—the very substance—of Empire. I hardly need remind your Majesties, is not merely good laws and efficient administration—which no one can deny the Imperial government has always provided, but rather the intricate web of comitatus which binds citizenry to nobility, nobility to royalty, and royalty to the imperial throne. It is, moreover, the irrefragable testimony of history that the one factor most conducive to loyalty at all levels is a powerful standing army. To assure themselves of the people's unswerving allegiance, knights hire retainers, barons keep larger forces still, provincial monarchs maintain entire legions, and, to ensure the perpetual stability of this far-flung but united Empire, the Imperial Regular Army was established. However, gentlemen —" (and here the Turtle began to extemporize),"—it goes without saying that just as a royal legion must maintain a higher pitch of esprit-de-corps than the retainers of a mere baron, so the Imperial Regulars must be unequivocally the sharpest troops in the world if they are to serve their intended purpose. With no malice intended, and in full appreciation of the difficulties with which my successor has no doubt had to contend, still, in my objective professional opinion, to allow discipline among the Emperor's Own Troops to reach the state I've witnessed today, frankly gentlemen, is to court national disaster."

The Emperor pondered, chewing his mustache.

"However," continued the Turtle, "I have come before you today not to criticize, but to take whatever constructive action the available opportunities will permit. I make no effort to conceal my disappointment in learning that my former position is no longer open, but I shall consider it my duty, as a soldier and as a citizen of this great Empire, to fulfill to the best of my abilities whatever assignment his Imperial Radiance sees fit to entrust to me."

There was a stir through the Hall as the delegates marveled at this great-hearted gesture. They broke into spontaneous applause. The Secretary Royal let the ovation continue for the exact number of seconds provided for in the Rules of Order, then gaveled for silence.

"You leave Us no choice," said the Emperor, "but to reconsider Our first hasty pronouncement. We see now that We've grossly misjudged your intentions. Would that all Our officers had your spirit of loyalty and service! You shall certainly resume your command. Moreover, consider our past disputes settled in your favor: you shall have the knighthood!"

Nobly as the Turtle had behaved, the Emperor had still eclipsed him. The delegates stood up and cheered wildly. In accordance with the Rules of Order, the Secretary Royal allowed twice the usual time for this, since it was the Emperor himself they were applauding.

"Your Radiance's generosity leaves me at a loss for words," said the Turtle emotionally. "I only hope I may prove worthy. What can I say, except to pledge that I shall not rest until our great feudal heritage is safe from all its detractors."

He had made the same pledge on several previous occasions, but the delegates gave him another round of applause anyway. The representative from the Turtle's natal province, who had been jotting notes for the last few moments, now stood up.

"The throne recognizes his Majesty, the delegate from Eastern

Trogloditia," said the Emperor (for it was technically he who presided over a plenary session of the Hall, although the Secretary Royal did most of the work and all the thinking)

"Distinguished Majesties," said the delegate, reading from his notes, "since this gentleman, and I don't hesitate so to style him, for he'll soon be a noble. I'm sure, by imperial decree, even if this motion I'm about to make isn't carried, though I see no reason why it shouldn't be carried—since this gentleman, in my opinion, and I think in any sensible man's opinion, even though he isn't of noble blood, as far as we know, and notwithstanding certain perhaps irregular political activities in the past, in connection with the Dynamic Feudalist Party, as I think it's called—since he has proven himself a staunch supporter of the Empire's proud traditions, and since he is, further, one of the very few men in the Empire, at the present time, who is possessed of the several outstanding qualities of character which will enable him to restore the Emperor's Own Troops to their best fighting trim, and thereby forestall civil strife— that is, in plain language, to stamp out wrong-thinking—and also to repel, or maybe even deter, the threatened invasion from the North —who can, in a word, solve, or substantially mitigate, all the disquieting problems that have, of recent months, been weighing so heavily on all our minds—therefore, distinguished Majesties. I feel that we, the royalty of the Empire, in our capacity as representatives of the citizens, the people, of all the provinces—I feel that we ought to express our appreciation for all the Turtle has done, and will do, that we express this appreciation in a positive manner, as befits royalty, and temporarily suspend—or, to put it a little less harshly, that we make this single unique exception to—the time-honored tradition of constitutional feudalism whereby our forefathers, the authors of the Great Charter, undertook to protect civilization from the evils of social mobility, which has been the ruin of so many less civilized foreign countries, especially the republics, and, as his Imperial Radiance has suggested, confer upon this gentleman the title of Knight, even though he isn't demonstrably of noble blood, for I feel certain, and I'm sure I'm not alone in this opinion, that, in view of his conspicuous sterling qualities of honesty, loyalty, valor, and, above all, genius in military tactical strategy—I feel certain that, somewhere in his lineage, noble blood has somehow crept in and I further move—"

"We second that motion," said the Emperor.

The delegate from Eastern Trogloditia looked up from his notes, mumbled something, smiled broadly, and sat down.

"Begging your Radiance's pardon," said the Secretary Royal, "your Radiance is out of order. According to the Great Charter, as well as the Rules of Order, all motions of this nature must be made and seconded by the royalty in the Hall of Kings. The Emperor is strictly limited to the powers of edict and veto."

"Then the Great Charter must be amended," said the Emperor, "because it just so happens that We second this motion. It's a fact that we'll have to live with, even if We're obliged to amend the Great Charter by imperial decree."

"Once again, your Imperial Radiance is out of order," said the Secretary Royal. "According to the Great Charter—"

"We may even have to appoint a new Secretary Royal," snapped the Emperor. "These are times of crisis, and we can't afford to hamstring the Imperial Government with legalistic technicalities."

The Secretary Royal held his peace and recorded the amendment in the Archives. "It has been moved and seconded," he announced, "that the title of Knight. be conferred upon the Turtle, a commoner, thereby breaking with a very ancient tradition and setting a dangerous precedent. Needless to say, gentlemen. I sincerely hope there is further discussion before I'm forced to bring this to a vote. Might I suggest—unofficially, since I'm not a delegate myself—that it might be wise to appoint a committee to study the proposal."

He looked around, but no one else seemed to think it needed study or discussion.

"Is there anyone," he demanded, "sufficiently short-sighted and irresponsible actually to favor this unconstitutional innovation?"

There was such a roar of approbation that no one even heard the Secretary Royal say "all opposed?" though it could be assumed that he did say it, for he always followed the Rules of Order to the jot.

"Motion carried," said the Secretary Royal bitterly.

"Your Radiance, permit me this last-minute appeal to your better judgment: The Empire's last hope is for an Imperial veto."

"Even if We opposed the measure," said the Emperor loftily, "We would have grave compunctions about such high-handed interference with the workings of constitutional government. Now, it remains only to decide which of the royal delegates will knight the Turtle. It should be done today before he takes command of the Imperial Regulars."

He glanced around the Round Table. There was no delegate pretentious enough to claim the honor.

"My own preference," the Turtle put in, "would be his Imperial Radiance himself, even if it is somewhat unusual."

"That's out of the question," said the Secretary Royal. "It's not only unusual; it's unconstitutional. The Great Charter expressly states that knights are to be dubbed by kings."

"That's a point," the Emperor agreed. "We crown kings, and We might consider you for that someday if We ever annex another province, but first, you must become a knight. How about the delegate from your own province?"

The Turtle bit his lip. Much as he coveted the knighthood, and ready as he was to make minor concessions when he had won his main point, and more, a fief in the dry hills of Eastern Trogloditia was hardly to his taste. A happy thought occurred to him. He struck a dramatic pose.

"I shall serve the Empire," he pronounced with an air of perfect moral conviction, "and no one king. In such times as these, even our oldest and deepest ties must be subordinated to a greater loyalty."

No one could conscientiously take exception to that point. There was an uneasy pause, while the delegates whispered, stroked their beards, and looked troubled, "Then," said the Emperor with great presence of mind, "you must be knighted by all the kings in the Hall, and We doubt that anyone here will decline the honor."

A roar of unanimous approval met this wise suggestion, and the ceremony began at once. The delegates drew their swords and jostled for early turns at knighting the Turtle, while the scribes scribbled frantically to record everyone's oratory. The Emperor himself, in the prevailing potlatch atmosphere, gave him the honorary title of Potency, which for want of a worthy candidate had not been conferred for nearly two hundred years.

That evening, in the Bachelor Officers' Quarters of the Central

Arsenal, the Turtle's military colleagues had a party to welcome him back to the army. In recognition of the historic precedent he had set in attaining knighthood, they acclaimed him permanent chairman of the Dynamic Feudalist Party.

It was a day the Turtle would always remember with a feeling of worthwhile accomplishment.

INTERLUDE - THE SAINT

The Saint mounted a hillock and looked out over the plain. The Capital was still a day's journey beyond the horizon. He stopped for a moment and closed his eyes, more clearly to see what was hidden by time and distance.

In the Capital, the Turtle's sudden rise to greatness had been greeted throughout the city with spontaneous outbreaks of violent rioting, for he had never been popular among the lower classes. The uprising was in its second day and would last another day.

The Radicals might have been able to stir the riot into full-scale revolution, the Saint noticed, had anyone other than the Turtle commanded the forces of law and order. Under his able leadership, the Imperial Regulars would soon have the city quieted. The Saint saw that he would not arrive until after it was all over. Destiny had provided for his safety.

The Saint opened his eyes." I shall be just in time to help the Scarecrow," he said, and went on his way.

FIVE

THE SCARECROW

The fighting between Conservative soldiers and Radical mobs was heaviest in the slums, where the Scarecrow occupied a single room on the fourth floor of a crumbling tenement. He was only dimly aware of the rioting in the street below. He knew this uprising was disorganized and foredoomed, so it did not interest him. Besides, he was busy. His thin, fanatic face was tense with concentration as he stirred a bubbling crucible.

"Fire of Freedom!" he exclaimed, snapping his fingers." I'll call it that. The name is concise, descriptive, alliterative, and intriguingly enigmatic. Fire of Freedom it is!" He steadied his hands by resting his elbows on the table and measured one drop from a poisonously-smoking bottle. The crucible sizzled at the disturbance, but the Scarecrow stirred it to sleep again.

He gnashed his teeth at a sudden, painful recollection. "A nerve!" he snarled; "a nerve, a bone, a nerve, a tendon, a clot of blood! Small wonder she won't have you! what more can you pretend to be than ingredients for a witch's broth, while she can take her pick of all the men in the Empire?"

He sighed mournfully. "But at least I kept from thinking about her for nearly an hour, and that's almost a record."

He seized a bottle and hurled it violently across the room to smash against the wall, "Don't think about her, you blasted idiot!"

he screamed, "Think about the Cause! Think about the advancement of science and the liberation of the working classes; think about the downfall of the tyrants! Think about destroying the Turtle, or the Neutrals, or yourself, or the world! Think about anything but her!"

Turning back to his crucible, he found the neglected stirring rod had sunk and dissolved. He kicked over a basket and selected another rod from among the junk that spilled out.

"Think about doing something right!" he shrieked, smashing an alembic with his fist. "Something! Anything! One simple task done right, the first in your life that doesn't turn out to be a blunder!"

He resumed stirring. The contents of the crucible had begun to flicker with shifting patches of colored light. After a few minutes, the Scarecrow added another drop from the smoking bottle and then a nugget of metal, which glowed balefully and had to be handled with tongs.

"Work," he muttered, "Work till your mind's too numb to visualize her face. Forget her until after the Revolt, when you've become famous," With his rod, he lashed viciously at a rack of test tubes. "And your well-heeled rivals have been guillotined!" The test tube rack overturned. There was a blue flash and a cloud of smoke. The Scarecrow ignored the smoke, and it rose to the ceiling to mingle with the other noxious effluvia he had recently created.

"With a tyranny to overthrow and a new world to build, she tells me I should spend my time trying to make gold. Even if it were possible, could gold win a revolution? The Neutrals think so, but they'll be disabused of that when the Fire of Freedom is unleashed!"

Toward morning, the rioting began to subside. Downstairs, the landlord, a Neutral by affiliation, peered out the boarded window. "I think by noon it might be safe to go out," he told his wife.

"Don't bank on it," the slattern replied. "Those Radicals just ran out of loose cobblestones to throw and moved on to the next street. They'll be back."

Their visitor, a fellow Neutral and a professional activist for the Party entered the kitchen. He had been trapped in the building three days before by the outbreak of the fighting and had deemed it wise to stay undercover for the duration. He had put the time to good use by spying on the Scarecrow.

"How's he doing?" asked the landlord.

"Splendidly," said the visitor. "I think he's about to pronounce it operational. It's quite a discovery: something like self-propelled naphtha, that selectively hunts down Conservatives."

"How's that possible?"

The visitor sat down at the table. "I don't have the technical background to understand much of his ranting," he said. "All I've gathered is that phlogiston, in the presence of certain catalysts, will form an unstable compound with caloric. The atoms of caloric retain their self-repulsive property in a compound, so the stuff diffuses rapidly. It would lay waste the countryside, except it contains traces of electrum, which has a strong affinity for noble blood. Just toss a capsule of this into the street, and poof! Every aristocrat in town goes up in smoke. Commoners aren't touched."

"That's really astounding," said the landlord.

"That's only part of it. Alloyed with small amounts of iron, it seeks out only soldiers; alloyed with quicksilver, only intellectuals; with gold, only the wealthy."

"My word," said the landlord.

"By varying the trace components according to well-established laws of alchemistic affinity, he'll be able to wipe out entire armies, or only the officers, however, he chooses. He believes he can vary the formula so the stuff will attack certain income classes or all members of certain professions."

"Say, this could be serious," said the landlord. "What about members of a specific political party?"

"He's got the Conservatives zeroed in. I guess he could wipe out any other party, too, once he works out the metallurgic affinities."

"Yes, it could really be serious. Consider the Scarecrow's pet hatreds: creditors, landlords, Neutrals... Are you sure you can get the formula away from him?"

"Positive. Just leave it to me. He may be a genius in his own specialty, but in everyday matters, he's a total dunce. I've got him convinced I'm a Radical myself."

"How did you manage that?"

"It wasn't hard. He jumps to conclusions. Just mention the words 'tyranny' or 'corruption' in almost any context, and you probably won't even have to tell him any direct lies. Getting the formula —and all the capsules he has—won't take five minutes."

The landlord rubbed his hands. "Our next Emperor will be a Neutral," he predicted.

"Just so we don't let his Radical confreres beat us to it," the visitor cautioned. "I'll have to keep checking on him."

The slattern brought a pot of hot tea, and they settled down to await developments.

SIX

THE SCARECROW AND THE SAINT

By the time the Saint arrived in the Capital, the uprising had been crushed, harsh new laws had been enacted by an emboldened government, and a dozen Oppositionist ringleaders had been hounded, foxed, or ferreted out of hiding by the Turtle's military police and bundled off to prison.

By that time, also, the Scarecrow had learned that the new owners of his formula were members of the wrong cause. Violent emotional crises were the Scarecrow's normal state of mind, but in relative terms, this setback brought on one of the most shattering psychic explosions to date, of which the external symptoms were only one aspect. He went into an extended frenzy of self-condemnation, pacing the floor, tearing his hair, shouting curses, and stopping every fifteen minutes from battering the door with his fists, beat his head on the wall, or break glassware. His neighbors were justly annoyed, but pounding on the wall educed no reaction one way or the other, and no one dared to disturb him in person.

The pacing footsteps paused for a moment, and the Scarecrow's neighbors held their breath and listened.

"This has gone far enough!" screamed the Scarecrow.

"Too far! Much too far! I can't stand it any longer! I can't bear to make another mistake! This final act, at least, will be done properly—I'll tell this execrable world exactly what I think of it!"

He rummaged around for a quill and a sheet of paper and found neither. He ground his teeth and swore, and broke a few crocks and bottles to restore his equilibrium, then made another disorderly search for writing materials.

"I can't do anything right! I can't even destroy myself right! All right, so I'll do it wrong!"

He burst through the door, reeled down two flights of stairs, fell headlong down the third flight, picked himself up, and stood on the landing clutching the banister.

"Get a grip on yourself!" he shouted at the empty hall. "If you break a leg, you can't get to the river, and some idiot will probably be stupid enough to splint it for you!"

He dashed out into the street. It was nearly midnight. Rain was falling. The Scarecrow set out for the river at a run, his wooden sandals clattering on the stone pavement. He met two soldiers who were patrolling the streets to enforce a newly-imposed curfew and ignored their orders to halt. They pursued him for a few blocks, but they were encumbered by their armor, and he outdistanced them easily.

Meanwhile, the Saint had arrived at the bridge with a few minutes to spare. He stood waiting in the rain and watched the swift, turbulent water.

"Death is the only release," he mused; "blessed oblivion is the final solace for all our grief, and, for a mere human being, the only attainable aspiration. How unfair it seems that some must strive so much longer than others to attain the same ultimate reward. Truly, the ways of Destiny are strange to those who do not understand."

Presently the Scarecrow arrived, his ill-fitting scholar's robe flapping as he ran. He stumbled down the incline onto the stone bridge and lurched to the railing, where he stopped to rest for a moment, breathing heavily, before his final plunge. The Saint approached.

"A bone," the Scarecrow was muttering between gasps, "a nerve, a thatch of sooty straw, a nerve, a ligament, and the greatest scientific intellect this ingrate world has ever lost."

"Salve," greeted the Saint gently. "*Pax tecum.*"

The Scarecrow jumped a cubit into the air and whirled, poised to run or fight. When he saw it was only a holy man, he turned back to the railing to stare into the swirling water.

"You must not go through with this, my son," said the Saint.

"Go through with what?" the Scarecrow challenged.

"You have come to escape your destiny," said the Saint reproachfully.

"Leave me alone."

"I want to help you, my son."

"I'll help myself."

"Please be reasonable. I must preserve you for your greater destiny, which is not at all as you imagine."

The Scarecrow snorted disgustedly. "You're too late. This is my destiny: the final idiotic blunder to end a lifetime of blunders."

Postponing suicide, he turned to confront the Saint's kindly brown eyes with his own two staring hollows of madness. "So you want to help me," he sneered. "Do you think a destiny would do me any good? My only graces are my intellect and education, and even if I could put them to use without blundering, what would my love want with a nerve and a bone and a nerve, sheathed in moldy parchment, wrapped in a rag, and befittingly thatched with dead moss?"

His voice dropped to a rasping growl. "All she wants is money. Some self-righteous blockheads—I'm talking about you, so listen carefully—would deem this reprehensible, but who am I to condemn her? To condemn? Hah! Who am I to think there could be any piffling blemish on the flawless sheen of her character? Get this clearly in mind, blockhead: Whatever she may plan, however, base her motive may seem by vulgar standards, the instant it comes into her mind, it's transmuted into something pure and fine. If it's money she wants for her favors, as happens to be the case, then money is a good and noble aspiration, and I'll strangle the cur who dares to disagree! Have I made myself clear?"

"I understand," said the Saint. "The moral doctrine of the Established Faith has many exceptions, and your case is one of them."

Somewhat mollified, the Scarecrow sighed and turned back to the guardrail. "What makes this point of view so difficult, sometimes, is that I haven't had the price of a square meal in over a month, let alone the toll to her affections." He leaned on the rail and covered his face with his hands.

"Azaza is not the whole meaning of your destiny," the Saint replied in soothing tones. "You have much to live for."

The Scarecrow looked up angrily and turned on the Saint again. "Much to live for! What else is there? Perhaps you mean the endless alchemistic busywork with which I struggle to blot out an ineradicable anguish—or are you driveling about the overthrow of the tyrants? That's where the real meaning of my life becomes apparent: everything I do is wrong! Unerringly, without exception, each of my loftily-inspired projects turns into a laughable mistake! Everything I touch blows up in my face! Just yesterday, an invention over which I'd toiled for months fell into the hands of the Neutrals, my sworn enemies, within minutes after I had it perfected! It would have been the Opposition's hope of defeating the Turtle and establishing a tolerable social order; now the Neutrals will seize power, and we'll be worse off than ever! But that's only one blunder among a multitude! The Turtle himself is invincible because of my stupidity! Years ago, I cast a cuirass from an alloy I discovered, which had the property of imbuing its wearer with almost superhuman leadership ability and prowess in battle. I sold it to a warrior, dirt cheap because he talked like a wrong-thinker and gave me the impression he'd use his invincibility to challenge the ruling classes. I even trusted him for part of the pittance I asked. Where's that double-crossing wrong-thinker now? In the Central Arsenal, commanding the forces of black, reactionary right-thinking! The crowning humiliation is that Turtle still owes me forty crowns; he's completely forgotten it, and I can't even go to claim it—if he remembers the debt, he'll remember me and have me arrested as a subversive! Even my enemies of the Neutral Party were able to organize an effective political faction because of shibboleths I coined myself! Their slogans—their whole ideology— is nothing but an absurd exaggeration of a metaphysic I published myself before I realized the damage it could do when perverted by warped minds! It's always the same! The theme of my destiny—the destiny you want to save me for—is one crushing defeat after another, without even the good fortune to be killed by my own blunders and thus spared from further blundering! Every dream turns to hallucination! Every word I utter turns into a lie, believed by all the wrong people! Evil fortune finds flaws in my most careful plans! I betray everything I believe in! If I discover a panacea, it breeds a pestilence! If I brew a poison, it cures some dread disease! If I don a cloak, there's always a loop or a button too many, and if I put on a pair of gloves, they're both for the left hand!"

The Scarecrow choked and could not go on, though he had apparently just gotten off to a good start. His eyes rolled. He leaned on the guardrail, racked by a fit of consumptive coughing. Overcome with grief and frustration, he sank to the pavement, where he sat with his head in his arms, sobbing, coughing, and cursing.

The Saint made a gesture of benediction over him. "You will bear the burdens of your life and your madness for your allotted time," he said, his voice vibrant with heartfelt sympathy. "Take comfort from my assurance that the damage you do proceeds from Destiny, and not from any evil in your own heart, for evil has no meaning in cosmic terms. Have courage, for your fortune is destined to change, someday."

Without looking up, almost absent-mindedly, the Scarecrow unleashed a torrent of appallingly brutal maledictions, borrowing freely from heathen cosmologies and classical literature. The Saint regarded him with infinite compassion and, of course, let it all pass. He wanted to comfort the Scarecrow further, but it was necessary to the Plan of the Universe that some things be withheld from the unenlightened. Apologetically he offered his blessing and sorrowfully turned away, leaving the Scarecrow exploding interminably on the bridge.

After a while, the Scarecrow calmed down. He got up and sat for an hour or so on the railing, staring down at the water and trying to work up enough nerve to jump in. Rain-soaked through his robe and drenched him, and streamed from his hair to dilute the tears coursing over his haggard face. He had lost his resolution.

He finally gave up and stumbled back to his tenement, where he managed to sleep for a few hours.

SEVEN

THE PATRIARCH

His Reverence, the Patriarch of Kalopolis, sat at the writing-table in his library, sipping vodka and fruit juice and gazing pensively at the flickering lamp. The rain had stopped, and the low-pressure area had floated northward toward the Capital. The sky was clear, and moonlight streamed in the Patriarch's window to make a pool of cold light on the floor, contrasting subtly with the warm glow of the lamp.

The Patriarch discovered he was out of vodka and tapped the gong. He waited five seconds and another five seconds. He was about to sound the gong again when Melli finally appeared. She was in her nightgown, and she looked tousled and sleepy.

"Asleep, eh?" said the Patriarch," I wondered what took you so long."

Melli nodded and rubbed her eyes.

"Sorry I bothered you," said the Patriarch sarcastically, "but now that you're up anyway, see if there's more of this in the cellar. I'm fresh out."

Melli picked up the empty bottle, glanced at the label, and vanished. She was back in three seconds with a fresh bottle of vodka, which she opened and set on the table.

"What time is it, anyway?" asked the Patriarch. Melli held up three fingers.

"That late? No wonder you were in bed. I've had things on my mind, and the hours slipped by."

Melli looked sleepily curious.

"My disciple," the Patriarch explained. "You remember him—that boy who was here a few days ago, just back from the mountains. Refused any refreshment except a glass of water, which, come to think of it, he never touched. He warned me of a Cataclysm that's coming up, and I haven't slept soundly since. It's no ordinary cataclysm, like the ones we usually get. The end of the world doesn't ordinarily amount to much more than a shake-up in high places, and we saints aren't supposed to bother about that sort of thing. This time, though, we're in for a real doozie."

The Patriarch mixed himself a drink, using about equal parts vodka and fruit juice.

"The kid sat there and calmly prophesied the downfall of the Empire and the Established Faith, then went on to admit he was to be the instrument."

Melli raised her eyebrows.

"That's right," said the Patriarch. "That boy, my own disciple, was sent by Destiny to destroy our Church and all civilization in the process."

The Patriarch drank. Melli cocked her head and looked puzzled.

"How should I know?" the holy man replied, "Why does the Universe do any of the idiotic things It does? When I answer that one. I'll start a church of my own. What is the Plan, and whom or what does it benefit? Not us; that much we know. If I thought this was all for humanity's ultimate good. I could take it philosophically, but we humans are microscopic motes in an infinite Cosmos, and our welfare's proportionally important. The Church is to be destroyed, and I'm to join the ranks of the unemployed. The Empire will fall apart, and the peace and quiet we've enjoyed these last ten centuries will end. For some reason, these things are necessary to the Plan."

The Patriarch refilled his goblet. Seeing that he needed company. Melli gestured at a chair.

"Sit down, by all means," said the Patriarch. "Never be formal with me unless there's someone around to impress. Have a drink."

Melli crinkled her nose and shook her head. She brought the chair closer and perched.

"I guess this stuff is a mite strong," the Patriarch admitted. "The heathen Muscovites drink mostly for effect. I don't usually care for vodka myself, but lately, I've needed something to settle my nerves heh heh. What was I talking about? Oh, Destiny." He swirled the potion in his goblet and gazed fondly at the little heathen goddesses on top of the bookcase. "Good old heathens," he said. "They always placed far too much importance on the world and its inhabitants. They thought this was the center of the Universe. That's one reason I've always had a soft spot in my head for heathens: they believed in themselves. It was their greatest strength, as well as their greatest weakness. Well, their day is past, in this part of the world. The squabbling heathen sects all fell apart, destroyed by their own self-contradictory doctrines, leaving the spiritual vacuum which our Church has filled so perfectly. The early prophets made sure nothing like that could ever happen to our Church. They knew the dangers of the wishful and mystical thinking the primitive religions are founded on, and they carefully avoided it when they codified our doctrines. That's why the Established Faith is the first church in history to be founded on pure Truth. To be on the safe side, we recognized no deities other than the Universe Itself, Which obviously has a purpose and a Plan, but is completely indifferent to human beings."

The Patriarch was inadvertently quoting, with the proper gestures and intonation, from his own lecture outline of decades before, when he had been a professor of theological history at the Kalopolis Seminary. Melli was used to this; the Patriarch was still occasionally invited to address theological conventions and other learned gatherings, and he always rehearsed his talks to Melli.

"The early prophets' most important contribution to valid theological science," the Patriarch continued, "was, as you all know, the doctrine of Destiny, which the poor heathens haven't accepted to this day, although incontrovertible proof has always been, and will always be, right before their misbelieving noses. The Truth is too obvious, you see. Rejecting the obvious in favor of involved, sophistical theorization has always been typical of the heathen mentality, Contrast, if you will, the compelling simplicity of our logic: There is only one past, therefore only one future;

therefore, no alternative to absolute, deterministic predestination. How succinct it is, yet how unassailable! That what will be will be is as pellucidly self-evident as that what was was, and what it is. The only argument to these tautologisms is pure, tender-minded, wishful thinking. Our prophets, of course, were much too wise to be misled by wishful thinking. They wanted a true religion. Since they were determined open-mindedly to accept whatever Truth they found, inevitably, in the course of time, they discovered the path to enlightenment."

The Patriarch paused for refreshment, then went on: "The Singlefold Path, as we call it in modern times, may be very briefly summarized: You must accept Fate, and get your heart right with All There Is. You remember the past, more or less accurately to the extent that you accept it as immutable—that much is proven psychological fact. It follows, therefore, that when you learn to accept the future as immutable, you can remember the future as well as the past. Sounds simple, doesn't it?"

Melli shook her head.

"But it's not simple. It takes years of meditation, under close supervision—preferably in a damp, drafty monastery where there aren't any worldly distractions—before you're really in tune. You have to alter your most elemental drives and hopes by a conscious act of will to make them correspond with the will of the Universe. When you've accomplished this, however, you can put your natural tendency toward wishful thinking to good use instead of having to fight it. The motives of the laity conflict with those of Destiny, often as not, so that their wishful thinking is proverbially deceptive. We saints, on the other hand, have no desires but those of the Universe. Since we hope for what will inevitably happen, our wishful thinking is a reliable source of information. Nothing is hidden from us."

Melli tried to conceal a yawn.

"I take it you're not much interested in sainthood tonight," the Patriarch suggested.

Melli smiled apologetically and shook her head.

"And anyway, I've probably explained all this to you before, haven't I?"

Melli nodded.

"You'll admit, though, that the logical foundation of our

theology is perfectly flawless, and in this, the Established Faith is unique in the history of religion."

Melli nodded again.

"I've made my point, then," said the Patriarch. "And yet it's destined that this beautiful, all-embracing system of fact, logic, divine inspiration, and intellectual honesty must crumble. As a moral human being—which has nothing whatever to do with being a saint—I see no valid excuse for depriving the world of its first and only non-heathen religion. That's what's been robbing me of sleep. Melli. I have a great decision to make, and it's not easy to face. In fact, it's an issue I've been dodging for fifty years, ever since my enlightenment, by trying to be a saint and a human being at the same time. Unrealistic of me, I'm afraid. I've made an honest effort to bridge the chasm between the mundane and the spiritual, between Man and the Universe. Now it's caught up with me. There's a Cataclysm staring me in the face, and I have to take sides. Which side should it be?"

Melli looked anxious but carefully noncommittal. The Patriarch tossed off his drink and mixed a stronger one. His pale eyes have lost some of their blear and, despite the vodka or perhaps because of it, had taken on a strange glint.

"Never heard of a renegade priest, did you?" he asked sharply, "I don't mean a heretic—there's plenty of those poor neurotics. I mean a perfectly orthodox renegade, who uses his saintly powers to obstruct the Plan."

Melli shook her head emphatically and looked shocked. "Well, you're about to hear of one." The Patriarch grinned satanically. He drained another goblet of moral courage and picked up the bottle again. He was adding less fruit juice to the vodka each time.

"The way I see it. I have precious little to lose that I wouldn't lose just as fast by resigning to Fate, as I'm expected to do. I can't lose my sainthood; it's in the Scripture that a saint can never lose his powers once he's enlightened. On the other hand, if the Church falls apart. I'm out of a job, and that's a serious predicament for a man well past his prime."

The Patriarch paused and turned his gaze out the window to the moonlit garden, "Yes. Melli. I've talked myself into a decision, haven't I? Right now, I don't know how to go about all this, but as soon as I sober up, I'll know the answer just by thinking about it.

Enlightenment has its conveniences, as well as its burdens. The first consideration. I'm afraid that if I want to cut a very wide swath as a seer, I'll have to ease up on drinking, maybe for days at a time. It won't be easy, at my age, but I have no choice. Generations of saints and prophets have labored to make the Established Faith a perfect religion. I can't sit idly by and watch their achievements wiped out by a whim of Destiny! Even faith has limits! Maybe I'll see this all in a different light after I sober up and know the Truth again, but I doubt it; something tells me I'm going to fight this through to the end. What do you think? Melli? Isn't it worth a try?"

He glanced at Melli. She was sitting very quietly, with her head drooping and her eyes closed.

"Melli," said the Patriarch sternly.

The girl awoke, blinked, and tried to look attentive.

The Patriarch was on the point of saying something caustic, but he changed his mind. "You'd better go back to bed," he said. "Kids your age ought to get plenty of sleep."

Melli nodded gratefully, stood up, and was gone, too fast for the eye to follow.

"She never complains," mused the Patriarch. "Sometimes I wonder if I'm not imposing on her good nature. After all, what would I do without her? I'd have to talk to myself if I didn't have such a talented audience."

He chuckled and raised his goblet in a toast. "To Mellisuga-helenae," he proclaimed, "the fastest girl in Kalopolis, and the easiest to get along with."

He thought for a moment, still holding the goblet aloft. "And to the Established Faith; may it be preserved from the Power to Which it's so thanklessly dedicated."

He downed the drink, which by then was almost pure vodka, set down the goblet, and stood up. He blinked, grabbed the edge of the table, and sat down again hurriedly, "Whee haw!" he commented. "I'll stick to civilized drinks from now on, nerves or no nerves!"

He sat still for a while, gently rocking his head from side to side. "Anyhow," he said thickly, thumping his fist on the table, "my mind's made up, and that's half the battle. Truth is worth all sacrifices! The Church must be preserved! Let my disciple make prophecies till he's blue in the face; this is total war! I'll show that punk a trick or two yet, or I'm not the Patriarch of Kalopolis!"

He sighed tragically and sniffled. "My boy," he said, as a tear trickled over his sunken cheek. "My own disciple—destroyer of the Church."

Presently he fell asleep with his head on the table.

EIGHT

THE SCARECROW

At the first peep of daylight, the Scarecrow awoke with a start. "I've got it!" he cried, springing from the straw mattress. "There's an answer to the Fire of Freedom, and to the Turtle as well! We're not beaten yet!"

He took a piece of charcoal from the sack by the stove and began to sketch a diagram on the floor. "The Opposition can't fail, with a weapon like this. I'll call it simply the Figure, and everyone who sees it will be obsessed with devotion to its owner. When I show it to Azaza, she'll fall at my feet. When the Neutrals see it, they'll instantly renounce their misplaced loyalty and support the Cause. When it's borne before the victorious legions of the Opposition, the tyrants' hirelings will be too overcome with love to lift their swords against us. Mounted on a pedestal in the Imperial Citadel, it will radiate peace and brotherhood to all the civilized world and bring on a golden age."

He scrabbled through books and scrolls for bits of technical data, covered the floor with charcoaled calculations, and gradually affixed details to his original rough design until it was a wondrous sprawling tangle of circles, angles, dots, arrows, broken lines, coils, condensers, resistors, scribbled words, numerals, and mystic symbols. When the whole plan was clear in his mind, he jumped to his feet, his eyes glittering with renascent obsession.

"Peace!" he screamed, "Peace! Love! Brotherhood! It will work; it has to work; every principle is sound! This is the destiny the holy man prophesied—the work of my life—the greatest alchemistic achievement of all time! But I won't build it here and have it stolen by my enemies. I'll go far away."

After carefully obliterating the diagram, he dashed out to pawn what little he had of value and returned with a few crowns in cash. He piled his books, bottles, tools, and crucibles on the bed, drew together the corners of the blanket, and tied the bundle with a piece of twine. He caught the first coach out of town, heedless of its destination, and rode most of the day, scheming and fidgeting. When he had used up as much money in carfare as he thought he could afford, he dismounted in a small river town a few leagues north of Kalopolis. He found a stuffy garret he could rent for nearly nothing, moved in, unpacked the bundle of alchemical equipment, built a fire in the stove, and went furiously to work.

NINE

AZAZA AND THE TURTLE

Azaza enjoyed great renown, not only among those who could afford her but among men in every walk of life, throughout the province and beyond. Among the rich, there were legions of satisfied yet insatiable clients. Among the poor, liars made her their favorite topic. Among the literati, hack authors enshrined her as a stock heroine. Among esthetes, she was a preoccupation; there were more contemporary paintings of her than of all other subjects combined, and every poet in the Capital had dedicated sonnets to her. No poet or writer could ever hope to reduce her to words and phrases, but they were undaunted by repeated failure. In the few short years, Azaza had been in clear public focus, several hundred sizzling adjectives had been newly coined and added to the language.

Her success was great, but her ambition was boundless. Her motivating dream was to model her life on that of Theodora, but, lacking Theodora's subtlety, Azaza simply strove to add more and wealthier members to her circle of admirers. Although it was a long climb from her initial obscurity, in that stratified era, no single rung of the ladder had been especially difficult. Azaza had only to be seen at any sort of social gathering and take her pick of the men who flocked around her. If a particularly affluent prospect was inhibited by shyness or well-bred reserve from approaching her of his own accord, then a crooked finger or a fluttered eyelid always brought him at a sprint.

Still, in a city the size of the Capital, she could not be every-where or meet everyone, and it was precisely the men who were still out of her class that Azaza felt she had to ensnare, both for the sake of their own fortunes and as stepping-stones to still greater heights. The Supreme Commander of the Imperial Regular Army was just such a remote and lofty public figure, and he attracted Azaza's attention as soon as he returned to power. In addition to his impressive title and salary, the Turtle had ready access to the Empire's copious defense budget, which Azaza had not yet been able to tap except at low levels. His reputation for scrupulous honesty did not worry her much; many other men in her life had been too upright to loot the public coffers—before they got involved with Azaza.

Her siege began with a casual note, a dinner invitation at her house, with a judiciously-worded but unmistakable promise of additional entertainment. It was the sort of invitation of which most men dreamed in vain, yet Azaza waited several days and received no reply. Concluding that the note must have been lost in the mails, she wrote another and sent it this time by her own gateman. The gateman reported that he had definitely seen the Turtle open the letter and read it. Azaza confidently sent for a caterer and made arrangements for a lavish but intimate banquet, complete with music. Several more days passed, however, and there was no response from the Turtle.

This was very strange, almost frightening. Azaza wondered if the Turtle was seriously ill, or unbelievably bashful, or worse. She did not intend to let the matter drop, for not only were the fiscal prospects unusually attractive but also, in neglecting to come to her on his own. The Turtle had aroused Azaza's predatory instincts.

A probable explanation for his indifference was that he had never seen her. It was remotely possible that he had never even heard of her, for he was known to discourage unseemly private lives among his subordinate officers, who would therefore refrain from mentioning Azaza when the Supreme Commander was around; and the Turtle was a serious man, who seldom associated with anyone but other soldiers.

Somehow, then, she had to contrive to meet him personally.

She devoted a great deal of thought to the problem. The Turtle scorned all frivolous society and would certainly never be seen at the sort of debauch to which Azaza could expect an invitation. She would have to intercept him somewhere as if by accident.

After she had mulled over and abandoned several schemes, the perfect solution turned up. She learned from neighborhood gossip that his Potency occasionally retired from the pressures of his command to the Teahouse of the Three Moons, the quiet establishment just a few doors from Azaza's own house. Exposing the Turtle to a personal meeting, which could hardly fail to overwhelm him, was simply a matter of having her gateman watch the teahouse entrance, and, when the Turtle showed up, happening to drop in. The gateman sighted the Turtle that very day, and at an hour, Azaza happened to have free. Things were finally going her way again.

As Azaza entered the teahouse, she found her prey alone, for the early afternoon trade was slack. The Turtle was seated at a corner table, reading a thick book and sipping at a half-gallon of cow's milk. He was in full armor, for some reason, and his helmet was tilted back on his head to give his active mind adequate ventilation.

The helmet was the Turtle's sole vanity. It was gold-plated, elegantly plumed, and emblazoned with his newly-registered escutcheon, a field argent charged with averting snapping-turtle rampant sinister, holding a cutlass in one fore flipper and an "excelsior-banner in the other.

His elbow was on the table, and his ruggedly handsome face rested on his hand. He followed the print with the forefinger of his other hand, for it was deep reading. His high, intelligent brow was furrowed with concentration, and he did not look up when Azaza came in.

At her first sight of the Turtle, Azaza felt an odd little flutter near her heart, which she had never experienced before. She felt an inexplicable touch of shyness and was tempted to sit down and wait for the Turtle to speak first. Unfortunately, she was pressed for time. She had a series of appointments for the afternoon and evening, and it was imprudent to let jealous clients pile up in the vestibule.

Her first caller would arrive in an hour, which left time enough to ensnare the Turtle, but none to waste. Rationalizing that decorum would be hypocritical anyway, she approached his table.

As she drew near, she saw that the tome he was reading was entitled: *A Brief Introduction to the Metaphysics of Social Evolution in the Modern Civilized World.* Here was a conversation piece, believe it or not. Azaza had not read the book (she had leafed through it once and had found at least half of each page filled with footnotes, often in Greek, Arabic, or Sanskrit), but she knew the author well. He was one of her most devoted admirers: The Scarecrow.

As the Turtle turned a page, the slight movement of his hand set enormous arm and shoulder muscles in motion. Azaza's pulse-rate mounted, and she had to remind herself she was there on business.

"Excuse me, sir," she began, "but I happened to notice the book you're reading—"

The Turtle's mighty fist crashed to the tabletop. Dishes and utensils jumped, and there was a sound of hardwood cracking. He did not take his eyes from the page.

"If I've told you once," he roared, mistaking Azaza for one of the waitresses, "I've told you twenty times: Don't disturb me when I'm trying to improve my mind!"

The thunder rolled away. The Turtle went on reading, "Well, I'm sorry!" Azaza retorted hotly and stalked away. The Turtle came to the end of a paragraph just at that moment. Marking the place with his finger, he looked up just in time for a fleeting glimpse of Azaza's figure before she disappeared through the door. His eyes widened.

"Great goodness!" he gasped. A true soldier, he always had a ready oath. "Great merciful Zas! Who in the world was that?"

"Oh, that's Azaza," said a waitress, "the famous—mm—ha ha— the famous—well—"

The Turtle rose, with a glassy look in his honest gray eyes, and knocked the heavy oaken table heedlessly out of his path as he rushed to the door. He looked eagerly up and down the street, but Azaza was already out of sight.

He returned to the table in a daze and sank heavily into his chair.

"Water!" he ordered, "Bring me water, quickly!" Sensing the

emergency, they brought him a large bucket of ice-water, which it took two waitresses to carry. The Turtle lifted it easily in one hand, as a lesser man would raise a teacup, and poured it, steaming, over his fevered brow.

"So that's Azaza," he said. "Those letters—but I didn't know — why didn't someone tell me—great Zas—so that's Azaza. I'll be dashed. Thank goodness it's only a few days till the Summer Solstice; this is an opinion I've got to revise forthwith!"

TEN

AZAZA AND THE SAINT

Azaza returned to her own house in the height of dudgeon that no one but a woman scorned can ever approach.

"I'll fix him," she informed her gateman, as she cast a searing look back toward the Teahouse of the Three Moons. "I don't know who he thinks he is, but he isn't—or won't be for long. I'm not without influence."

"What has his Potency done, miss?" asked the gateman solicitously, locking the iron grill again.

"Never mind," snapped Azaza.

"I don't like to bother you with trivia when you're in this frame of mind," said the gateman, "but there's someone here to see you. He assured me he only wanted a minute of your time,"

"Your first duty as a gateman," said Azaza icily, "is to admit no one without an appointment. They all say they'll only be a minute —then just try to get rid of them."

"Not this one, miss—he's not a customer; he's a holy man. I told him you were out, and he prophesied you'd be back in exactly fourteen minutes and ten seconds. What could I do?"

"Oh...Well, if he's already waited fourteen minutes, then he can wait till I freshen up. What would a holy man want with me?"

"He didn't say. He implied, delicately, that I'm not worthy of knowing such things—as of course, I'm not."

"Who is?" said Azaza understandingly.

"Where is he now?"

"I had him wait in the garden."

"Good; maybe I can avoid him."

Azaza started for a side door of her house so that she would pass through as little of the courtyard garden as possible. At that moment, spiritual guidance was about the last thing she wanted.

"No man shouts at Azaza," she brooded; "I don't care who he is. His Potency hasn't heard the last of this—I have connections. I'll fix that overstacked slab of beef."

"So you will, my child," said the Saint from behind her.

Azaza whirled. "Will what?" she demanded, wondering how the holy man had found her so easily.

"You will successfully avenge your wounded pride," murmured the Saint.

"How do you know about that?" Azaza was irritated by the note of confidence in the Saint's voice and puzzled by the incongruously gentle tone in which he spoke of avengement. "How could you have found out about that so soon?"

The Saint smiled and spread his hands.

"We who are enlightened need not depend on the vagaries of hearsay," he replied, "for the Universe is omniscient, and we are Its emissaries. Much as it grieves me to say it, you will keep your pledge, for it is destined."

"But I love him," protested Azaza. "How can I harm the man I love?" Then she wondered why she had said it. She was strangely unable to meet the Saint's compassionate gaze.

"And what you do," the Saint added sorrowfully, "you must do with your own hands."

"What is it?" asked Azaza in panic, "What must I do?"

The Saint shook his head slowly, "Destiny will arrange for all things," he said; "I am not allowed to reveal the details of the Plan to the unenlightened. But please do not blame yourself for what you are about to do, for this tragic interruption of his Potency's career has been inevitable since the beginning of time, and we mere humans must not question Destiny, Farewell, my child. The blessings of the Universe be with you, and the task before you."

The color drained from Azaza's face as she caught the ghastly implication. She leaned faintly against a tree.

For the first time in her wicked life, the pure fire of love was burning amid the wreckage of her soul, yet even as this startling realization flooded her mind, she also knew she had to try to kill the Turtle, however little she now wanted to.

ELEVEN

THE SCARECROW

At that moment, many leagues away, three stories below the Scarecrow's workshop, the landlady gripped the edge of the kitchen table to steady her nerves and shot an accusing glare at her husband.

"There he goes again," she nagged. "My mother warned me not to marry a landlord, but how was I to know what I'd have to put up with?"

"He pays his rent," said the landlord defensively, "Times are hard, and we need the money, and I thought I'd never get that miserable garret rented."

From the attic above drifted a mournful howl: "A nerve! A bone! A nerve! A shred of parchment!..." The howl slid half a kilocycle up the scale and leveled off at a frenzied banshee scream: "Peace! Love! Brotherhood! Comfort to suffering mankind!"

The landlady closed her eyes and shivered. She was staving off a nervous breakdown from one minute to the next.

"All right," sighed the landlord. "I'll have an eviction notice recorded today and spring it on him first thing in the morning. I don't think he's quite as excitable when he first wakes up."

TWELVE

THE PATRIARCH

The Patriarch of Kalopolis, sober for once and in control of his saintly faculties, sat at his table with his eyes closed and watched the Saint, in the Capital, paying a ceremonious call on the Prime Ecclesiarch. His Saintliness, the spiritual leader of the entire civilized world, was incredibly old; he had lived to conduct funeral services for six emperors of the dynasty. He was also incredibly fat; he had long since outgrown a globular shape and had become almost a mound.

The Saint and the Prime Ecclesiarch talked for a long time. Their dialogue consisted of single words and brief sentence fragments, spaced at long intervals. The sparing use of words did not limit the range of their discussion, which delved exhaustively into every subject within human comprehension. Both men were saints, and both knew whatever they wished to know, merely by thinking about it. Single words or gestures to call various matters to each other's attention were all they needed.

The Patriarch of Kalopolis kept his eyes shut and watched them until he was bored beyond further endurance by a twenty-minute conversational lull. He opened his eyes and watched Melli, who was dusting bookshelves.

"Don't move so fast," he chirped.

Melli stopped dusting and looked puzzled.

"I enjoy watching you," the old lecher explained, "but you're too fast to keep track of. It makes my head swim."

Melli nodded and obligingly moved more slowly, though now she seemed a little self-conscious. The Patriarch leered for a while, but the problems at hand kept intruding on his more customary train of thought. He closed his eyes again.

"My disciple's coming right along with his Church-wrecking project," he reported, "No; let me amend that: at least he's off to a roaring start on undermining the Empire. He's stopped the Scarecrow from ending it all and put him to work on an ultimate weapon of some sort. I can't tell how that will fit in, exactly. Also, he's convinced Azaza she has to assassinate the Turtle, who's back in command of the Imperial Regulars. That was a dirty trick, destined or not! I can't tell how that'll fit into the Plan, either, but it looks serious."

He shook his head, as if it were a malfunctioning timepiece, "To tell the truth. I can't tell how much of anything's going to fit in. I can see distance now, but the future's still hazy, even though I'm stone sober. One thing I do know, without the benefit of saintly insight, is that the Empire's stability depends on the Turtle's good health. I've got to stop Azaza. I wonder how."

The Patriarch rubbed his forehead. "It's odd—I can see the future for most things, but it starts to blur when I focus my mind on anything concerning the Cataclysm. I've tried to see into the Prime Ecclesiarch's future, and my disciple's, and the Turtle's, and my own. All these futures seem to start fading out after a couple days, and a week from now, everything's blank. It's sort of frightening...I can tell the Church is in mortal danger, but I can't pinpoint the threat. It's almost as if Destiny were hiding Itself from me. That's a good sign, actually, because it means I'm dangerous, and that means I might be able to do some good."

He opened his eyes. "Standard battle-plan," he announced. "We'll fight Destiny in Its own element. Trivial stimuli, after a sufficient lapse of time, have earth-shaking consequences. 'Because of a nail, the shoe was lost,' so they say, and so on through an improbable but apparently predestined sequence of effects to the inevitable fall of the kingdom, 'all because of a horseshoe nail.' Something just as trivial might destroy the Church, or save it, or shape the fate of all human civilization. Let the statesmen and heroes posture as they will. Melli, in the last analysis, it's trivia that will change the course of history. My task, therefore, is to analyze those portions of the Plan of Destiny that involve this Cataclysm and introduce small, undetectable counter-stimuli that will run their courses before the Winter Solstice and undo my disciple's work. That won't be as easy as it sounds. One thing I've found out today—even if I can never lose my hard-won sainthood, the Universe can sure thin it out when It takes a mind to. My insight hasn't revealed a thing about practical manipulation. If I were on authorized Church business, it would be a different breed of cat."

The Patriarch reached automatically for his goblet, his drinking-arm still responding to half a century of habit. He looked irked when his fingers closed on empty air.

"Take my disciple, for instance," he went on. "That stiff can't possibly comprehend the forces he's setting in motion. The Universe does his thinking for him. If you wanted to plot a sequence of events with one hundred percent accuracy—and Destiny won't settle for less, believe me—you'd have to compute the exact position and velocity of every atom in creation and then trace the future positions of each one, instant by instant. 'Democritus's Method,' we call it, and it's a sort of in-group joke; no mortal mind could even begin such a project—it takes an Infinite Intelligence. My disciple is just following instructions on blind faith, like the devout stooge he is, but I'll have to do it the hard way. The figuring doesn't bother me so much, though—my boy's real advantage is that he doesn't have to disguise his activities. It's all very well for him to come right out and tell Azaza she has to snuff out the Turtle, but for a similar operation, I'd have to use a causality-sequence involving at least twenty stages to avoid detection."

The Patriarch mopped his brow with his sleeve. "And that, Melli is the prime consideration: I'd damned well better not get caught at this. I could handle the boy all right, ball of fire though he be, but if the Prime Ecclesiarch gets wind of what I'm up to..."

The Patriarch shuddered visibly. Melli paused in her work and looked worried.

"All my manipulations will have to be handled with the utmost circumspection. Imperceptible stimuli, at widely scattered locations, preferably far away from the Capital. It'll mean a lot of footwork for you. I'm afraid."

Melli shrugged. The distance was a matter of complete indifference to her.

"What would I ever do without you. Melli?" said the Patriarch warmly. "If I can count on you. I'll have a chance."

Melli blushed modestly and resumed dusting.

"Little causes, big effects," said the Patriarch, steepling his fingers and smiling evilly. "A purloined horseshoe nail, a coin on the roadway, a word in someone's ear, a dead fish in someone's bed —these are the weapons with which the real battles of history are fought...Well, the first thing an army needs is intelligence: I have to find out exactly what my boy plans to do."

He rose from the table and hobbled to his couch. Melli dropped her dust cloth and came to arrange the cushions for him. The Patriarch settled himself comfortably.

"I need company," he said; "sit down."

Melli seated herself diffidently on the edge of the couch. The Patriarch closed his eyes again for a better view of spiritual matters. Absent-mindedly he fondled the girl's thigh.

"Those two holies are still in conference," he narrated, "and neither one has said a word for half an hour. We saints aren't much for gab, you'll notice. That's one reason enlightenment began to pall for me once the novelty wore off. It takes all the spice out of conversation. There they sit, two pious minions of Destiny, with folded hands and downcast eyes, contemplating the beauty of the Plan and the details of our destruction. At least the boy is; I suspect old Lardbelly's dozed off. Yes, he has; he's snoring."

The watery eyes popped open. "Too bad the Prime Ecclesiarch's on Destiny's side. The kid doesn't worry me so much; I've got fifty years' experience over him, but if the Prime Ecclesiarch so much as happens to wonder what I'm doing these days, the jig's up. I'd have to stay sober for weeks at a time to outfox the holiest man in the Empire, and it's hard, at my age. I'm afraid our success depends on his Saintliness not happening to horn in. We'll have to operate by night, mostly, and at times like this when he's dead to the world."

He shut his eyes for a final check. "The old bullfrog is sound asleep. The boy's too polite to wake him, so we have a clear field until his feeding time. This is our chance to get started. No use watching those two anymore, and since my inner vision's so cloudy today. I guess we'll just have to fall back on the Scripture."

His eyes opened. "That's what the Holy Scripture's for. Melli. It's a guidepost in the wilderness, when we poor sinners stray from the path of saintliness and lose our way, Fetch me volume VII of the Book of Prophesy; that one's usually good for a few pointers."

He gave the thigh a parting squeeze. "And bring me a drink," he added. "I'm in bad shape. See how my hands are shaking? I haven't had a drink since before breakfast, and at my age, these excesses could be dangerous to my health."

THIRTEEN

THE TURTLE

When the Summer Solstice arrived, the Turtle did not attend the public festivities. Feigning a headache, he stayed in the almost-deserted BOQ, pacing the floor in great agitation and stepping out into the courtyard several times an hour to look at the sundial. At high noon exactly, he availed himself of his semiannual license to change his mind and fell desperately in love with Azaza.

Instructing his personal guards to disturb him for nothing short of Condition Red, he retired to the privacy of his quarters to compose a letter. He sat down at his table, took out a sheet of paper, stirred the inkwell, sharpened a quill, dipped it, thought for a moment, then wrote:

Dear Azaza:

He regarded the salutation critically and found it wanting both vividness and originality. He discarded that sheet, took out another one, and wrote:

Dearest Azaza:

He removed his helmet, scratched his head, and put the helmet on again. He read the words over a few times, pondering. The more he looked at them, the more he thought there was still room for improvement. Finally, he tore up that sheet and started anew.

My Dearest Azaza:

No, that would never do. Blushing, he carefully obliterated the words with drops of ink before he took another sheet of paper. Perhaps a more formal approach would be better, or at least safer.

Your Ladyship:

He nibbled the end of the quill. He knew perfectly well Azaza was not titled; this was meant as flattery—to be frank—but might it not be misconstrued? He squinted at it. Through his right eye, it looked like the compliment he intended but viewed through his left eye; it was decidedly sarcastic. He tried again.

Dear Miss Azaza:

That was a little better, but still much too formal, come to think of it, for the impassioned message he had vaguely in mind. The Turtle's lofty brow furrowed. He removed his helmet again and set it on the table, precisely at right-dress with the lamp and the inkwell. He chewed his quill and rumpled his curly black hair. Letters certainly were not his specialty, particularly love letters to a woman he scarcely knew. He wished he could stick to direct conversation, for which he imagined he had more talent. However, a personal meeting with Azaza would require strict secrecy and careful planning. Even in the grips of love, the Turtle was a soldier first and foremost, and his duty to the Empire was to keep his reputation unsullied. A letter would have to suffice, for the time being, and perhaps for a long time to come.

He put his helmet on again, squared his shoulders, cleared his throat, and began writing, neatly but rapidly.

Dearest Azaza:

It is earnestly to be hoped that I may be indulged an egregious lack of facility with the pen. The written word. I sadly regret, can hardly be deemed my forte. Notwithstanding this infelicitous ineptitude, it is nonetheless imperative that I devise some means wherewith to communicate an apology for my dreadful (although. I sincerely hope, not altogether unpardonable) blunder on the occasion of our initial encounter. It is among my darkest apprehensions that I may have irredeemably alienated your esteem before we have had suitable opportunity to cultivate even the most superficial acquaintance. Please believe my fervid assurance that I

. . .

THE TURTLE SWORE and tore the letter to shreds. Why in the name of Zas couldn't he write letters when he did so many other things so expertly? He brooded for a while, then re-inked his quill, took a fresh sheet of paper, and wrote:

The Office Of The Supreme Commander
Imperial Regular Army
Subject: Official Apology For Recent Case Of Mistaken Identity
Section I: Purpose And Scope A)

He added this to the growing heap in the wastebasket. He rose and paced gloomily around the room, automatically hitting pivot-points at each corner. He sat down at the table again, made a few more false starts, then wrote the day off as a loss.

He made a tour of inspection of all the guard posts, and bawled out several sentries for nothing at all.

FOURTEEN

THE SAINT AND THE SCARECROW

The Saint caught up with his destined appointments in the Capital, then detoured south to call on the Scarecrow, who already had his secret weapon half completed.

"How did you find me?" the alchemist asked when the Saint came in. "No one knew I was here."

"We, who are enlightened," the Saint explained, "have access to whatever information we need to implement the Will of Destiny."

"I see," said the Scarecrow. "Well. I'm glad of this chance to thank you for the favor you've done me. I actually owe you my life, not to mention the inspiration for this greatest of inventions."

He turned to the workbench and waved his soldering iron at the amorphous tangle of wires and metallic parts.

"The Figure," said the Scarecrow with mounting excitement, "will be the greatest contribution to world culture since fire or the lever. Once the tyrants are defeated, war and strife will be forever banished from the earth. It will mark the turning point in history, and I'll see to it that the chronicles of the new Empire give you your rightful due as the man who saved my life and made it all possible."

He glanced at the Saint and noticed that his enthusiasm was not shared. "What's wrong?" he asked, suddenly apprehensive.

The Saint sighed. "You must not put your faith in worldly

science, my son." Then he added," I have come again at the behest of the omniscient Universe."

"Oh?" said the Scarecrow suspiciously. "And what have you come to implement this time?"

"I have come to advise you that your invention will fall into the hands of the Neutral Party."

"Neutrals! Those vermin? I'm glad you warned me; I couldn't bear to have that happen again. How can I elude them?"

The Saint shook his head sorrowfully. "You cannot escape, my son. It is destined."

The Scarecrow stared at him, his eyes bulging wildly as the import sank in.

"No!" he gasped, dropping his tools and collapsing into a chair. "Destiny wouldn't do that! Not twice in one lifetime!"

"It is necessary," replied the Saint softly.

The Scarecrow rakes his bony fingers through his hair, breathing heavily.

"I won't finish it!" he shouted suddenly. "I refuse to work on it! The Figure can't be stolen if it's never completed!"

"It will fall into the Neutrals' hands," the Saint predicted dolefully, "in five days' time."

Relief crept into the Scarecrow's expression. "I can't possibly finish it in five days. It will take weeks!"

"You must believe me, my son. What is destined is an accomplished fact in the eyes of the Universe."

"I've no place to work," the Scarecrow quibbled. "Even if I could finish it in such an impossible hurry. I need a place to work, and the landlord's already evicted me." This was sheer hypocrisy; he had not given the eviction notice a second thought until this moment.

"You will be allowed to stay here," the Saint assured him. "I have spoken to your landlord."

The Scarecrow sprang to his feet considering violence, then thought better of it and paced the creaking floor.

"So I have to believe you," he conceded bitterly, "but why did you come here to torment me with prophecies? Do you think telling me this has made things any easier for me?"

"It is destined that the Neutrals shall seize Kalopolis," said the Saint. "They cannot do so without your invention. It will take time for them to learn how best to use it, and in order to have exactly as much time as they need, no more and no less, they must have the Figure by sundown five days from now. If I did not tell you this, you would continue to work at your normal pace, and the Figure would not be completed in time to play its destined part in the Plan of the Universe."

"Then it's not destined at all—this is just an elaborate scheme of yours!"

"It is destined, my son, for I was destined to say everything I have said and am saying, and I have no power to alter Destiny."

The comforting tone was no solace to the Scarecrow. He dropped back into his chair and covered his face with his hand. With the other hand, he pointed peremptorily at the door. "Get out! "he ordered." I refuse to work on the Figure! I defy the Universe, and I defy you! Get out!"

The Saint turned to leave.

"Wait!" shouted the Scarecrow. "One question! Destiny has set me an impossible task. What are the consequences if I fail?"

The Saint paused at the door. "There are no consequences," he said kindly. "Reward and punishment are the ways of mankind, not of the Universe. You cannot possibly fail."

FIFTEEN

AZAZA AND THE TURTLE

The Solstice passed, and several days followed. Azaza canceled all her appointments and hid from the world, refusing food. Her emotional turmoil worsened day by day, as she was inwardly torn between an overpowering urge to murder the Turtle and a burning love for him, which grew more painfully urgent with every passing hour.

Vainly she fought the full obsession. She tried to distract her mind by reading, but the only book at hand was the Scarecrow's *Brief Introduction to the Metaphysics of Social Evolution in the Modern Civilized World*, and the bewilderment it engendered in her undisciplined mind further reduced her defenses against recurring thoughts of killing. She gave that up and spent some time practicing what little sorcery she had learned from her mother. This helped to distract her, but she soon realized where such things could lead when the obsession finally conquered her—as it obviously would.

It was with a somewhat reduced feeling of tension—comparatively almost relief—that Azaza made her decision. She would compromise. She resolved she would at least kill the Turtle honestly and naturally, without recourse to black arts. For several hours after that, she procrastinated resolutely, but in the end, there was nothing she could do about it. The will of Destiny was manifest, and she had to go murder the Turtle.

Late that night, she put on a dark, hooded cloak of the style affected by spies and assassins and slipped out a back gate into the moonlit street. She had no particular plan and was too upset to devise one; her thoughts were in boiling confusion. She trusted to improvisation, and to Fate, whose idea it was in the first place.

The streets were deserted, and Azaza met no one until she reached the Imperial Citadel and rounded the enormous enclosure to the gate of the Central Arsenal. The drawbridge was down. This ostensible contempt for surprise attack was one of the Turtle's innovations, for he felt it would serve to unsettle seditious elements and bolster public morale.

To get into the Central Arsenal at that hour on legitimate business would have involved hours of red tape, but Azaza had only to ask for the Captain of the Guard, whom she knew quite well. She had him helplessly in thrall, not only with her charms but also with the threat of blackmail; some of his tastes were a little unusual. When the Captain of the Guard saw who had asked for him, he turned flaming red, then ash gray. When Azaza insisted without explanation that he let her into the Arsenal, his sense of duty prevailed for a while, and he somehow found the courage to stall. Azaza threatened him sweetly. The Captain of the Guard hemmed and hawed, vacillated, quibbled, moaned softly, chewed his lip, perspired, and finally ordered the sentries to turn their backs while he let Azaza in through the wicket.

She got past several more checkpoints by telling various stories, and the fact that she was already inside the main gate made her lies plausible. She did not know the layout, but like all military installations, the Central Arsenal had a profusion of fingerposts at every turn, by which Azaza quickly found the Bachelor Officers' Quarters. There were guards at the entrance. Weary of argument and delay, Azaza avoided them by scaling the low, vine-covered wall of the inner courtyard, and she was not interfered with again until she reached the main corridor of the BOQ. She wandered through the building, wondering what to do next until she encountered a guard. He was a beardless recruit, so insignificant a threat that Azaza ignored him until he actually challenged her.

"Halt!" the recruit recited, "Who Goes There?" Azaza turned, somewhat surprised at the stripling's effrontery.

"Not so loud, churl," she said imperiously, assuming the accents of the nobility, "I'm looking for the apartment of his Potency the Supreme Commander."

In an offhand act of psychological warfare, she casually loosened her cloak as if it were a little too warm in the building. None of Azaza's dresses were less than obscene in style, and the one she wore under the cloak, except for strategic fluffs and baubles, fit her like paint. The youth was instantly entranced.

"Are you deaf?" Azaza asked sharply. "I asked you for directions."

"I'm—I'm sorry, ma'am," the guard stammered absently, fixing his eyes involuntarily on Azaza's torso, "but you're not allowed—no one's allowed—that is. I'm not allowed to allow—"

"What are you gawking at?" snapped Azaza, who had no objection but was currently concentrating on imperious effect. "Don't you know it's illegal for a commoner to leer at a lady?"

The guard's gaze snapped to an indefinite point on the wall. "Yes, m' lady," he said, gulping. He doubted that there was any such law, and he could not imagine what a noblewoman would be doing in the Bachelor Officers' Quarters, but his three weeks in the army had taught him not to take chances.

"Now direct me to his Potency's apartment," Azaza repeated.

"My orders, m'lady—"

"Shall I turn you in for insolence, as well as impropriety?"

"His Potency's quarters are at the end of the first corridor to your left, m'lady," said the guard hurriedly.

Azaza moved away in the direction indicated. As soon as she had turned into the lateral corridor, the recruit, remembering his General Orders, dashed to report to the Corporal of the Guard.

Outside the Turtle's door stood two personal bodyguards, who snappily drew their swords and stepped out to block Azaza's progress. Azaza was not familiar with military organization, but she was able to size up these new adversaries by their faces, if not by their chevrons. One had the dull eyes and slack features of a private first class. The other's face reflected the pragmatic animal cunning of a sergeant.

"Halt!" chanted the sergeant and the PFC in unison. "Who Goes There?"

"Why hello, sergeant," said Azaza cordially. "Haven't we met somewhere before?" This was unlikely, but the approach was tried and proven.

"That we have," said the sergeant, to Azaza's surprise.

"Next question is, what are you doing in the BOQ at this hour? As far as that goes, what is any woman doing anywhere in the Central Arsenal at any hour?"

Azaza hastily changed tactics. "I'm here on official business," she said.

The sergeant laughed merrily. "That's mighty likely, Azaza," he said. "I'm sure your business is official."

Azaza did not know him from John Q. Adams, but he evidently knew her, besides which he was not reacting normally to her physical presence.

"His Potency has sent for me," said Azaza frantically. "Stand aside!"

"Wonders won't quit, will they?" replied the sergeant with considerable glee. "For a breach of regulations like bringing a woman in here, he'll have to court-martial himself. I never thought I'd see the day when his Potency took up breaking his own regulations. This would make a top-notch story to spread around the NCO club, except I seem to recall the famous Azaza can't flap her pretty little forked tongue without lying. I don't know how you got this far, but from here, you go straight to detention. You're under arrest."

Azaza remembered the sergeant now. They had met once when the military police had seen fit to question her about the political opinions of one of her clients.

"On what charge?" she demanded.

"Espionage," said the sergeant cheerfully." Ask me another."

This man, Azaza remembered, was immune to feminine logic, preferring a military logic of his own. This was an occasion for drastic measures.

"I warn you, sergeant," she said, "you're making a mistake. This doesn't amuse me in the least!"

"I don't guess it does," replied the sergeant unfeelingly.

He produced a pair of handcuffs, which, as an MP, he always carried tucked in his sword-belt.

"All right, sergeant," said Azaza, as she pulled off her cloak and dropped it on the floor, "you've had your chance to be reasonable."

The sergeant began to look worried as Azaza kicked off her sandals and loosened her sash. Her dress came open, and she had nothing on under it. The PFC dropped his sword and quickly stooped to retrieve it. Azaza slipped out of her dress and dropped it on top of the cloak.

"You pick up those clothes and put 'em back on!" ordered the sergeant, point with his sword at the heap. "What kind of...?"

At this point, there was a clattering of sandals, and the Corporal of the Guard, with drawn sword, rushed around the corner, followed closely by the recruit, also with drawn sword. The two slid to a halt and stood gaping.

Azaza glanced around contemptuously at the intruders, then, smugly and deliberately, while the four soldiers stood in jaw-dropping stupefaction, she peeled off her skin and stepped away from it, completely invisible.

Four swords dropped from four nerveless hands and clattered noisily to the mosaic floor.

Invisible and intangible, Azaza slipped around behind the sergeant, picked up one of her discarded sandals and poised it for a sharp blow, then lifted off the sergeant's helmet and clouted him. He collapsed, mostly from fright, Azaza plucked off the PFC's helmet next, but the soldier recovered his meager wits just before she struck. He emitted a hoarse cry, shouldered the recruit and the Corporal of the Guard roughly aside, and sprinted down the corridor, shouting something about witchcraft. Seconds later, the other two soldiers followed the PFC, and Azaza was alone.

As the terrified shouts died away in the distance, other sounds arose. These were the queries of sleepy officers, opening their doors in nearby corridors to see what the disturbance was. The invisible Azaza hastily set down the PFC's helmet, gathered up her skin, her dress, and her cloak, tiptoed into the Turtle's quarters, and bolted the door. Feeling a little chilly, she paused inside the door to put on her skin and her clothing. She noticed she had forgotten her sandals, but already there were voices approaching, and it was too late to go back.

The Turtle slept like a man with an immaculately clean conscience. The shouting in the corridor had not disturbed him, although it had apparently roused the rest of the BOQ.

Azaza jumped in fright as a gentle, deferent knock sounded at the door just behind her. She had no time to spare if the Turtle was to be murdered before the growing clamor awakened him. Guided by the Turtle's placid snores, she crossed the stark, spartanesque sitting-room to the door of the sleeping chamber and entered silently.

The officers were knocking more urgently. "Your Potency?" someone called, "Your Potency, are you there?" Just then, the moon, unveiled by the broken, shifting clouds, flooded the room with light. It revealed the Turtle himself, supine beneath a light-weight army quilt, his profile silhouetted in the moonlight. His sword and helmet rested on a footlocker by the bed.

Until that moment, Azaza had not had time to think about her own inner conflict of motives, but at the sight of the Turtle asleep, love rushed back into her heart. She remembered with agony just how little she wanted to go through with this grisly adventure.

Moving in a grief-stricken daze, she grasped the Turtle's sword. The heroically-proportioned weapon was all she could lift with both hands. With her head reeling and tears in her eyes, Azaza raised the sword, aimed it at the Turtle's muscular neck...and faltered. With success so close, her resolution vanished. This was her beloved, whom only a careless oath and a cruel whim of Destiny had forced her—of all people—to kill.

She suddenly realized with clutching terror that she had made no provision for escape from justice, and once the frightful deed was done, her own life would be very short. But would that really matter, with the Turtle dead?

She stood with the vorpal blade poised while her heart pounded, her breath caught in her throat, and tears filled her eyes. She could not do it.

And yet she had to. It was destined.

"Forgive me, my love," she cried piteously. "Why is it my destiny to do this thing? Why must I be the one to kill the man I've so recently learned to love?"

The Turtle's eyelids opened. A cloud covered the moon.

Azaza cut short her lamentations, and, pressed on by an

impulse much stronger than her own will, she closed her eyes and swung the sword.

There was a loud clang of steel on steel, and the sword rebounded.

"Now what on earth...?" said the Turtle. Azaza opened her eyes. The Turtle threw the quilt aside, sprang out of bed, and snatched the sword; Azaza's surprise phased immediately into ecstatic joy. She had often heard it said that the Turtle was called the Turtle because he never removed his armor except to bathe. The rumor was true, after all. The Turtle slept in his armor.

"Great Zas!" exclaimed the Turtle, blinking. "A woman? In my quarters? Of course, I'm dreaming." He put the sword back on the footlocker.

"I came to kill you," said Azaza candidly, with a sigh of relief, "but I've failed, thank heavens! Destiny can't blame me for having tried and failed."

"Beg your pardon?" said the Turtle. "Who are you? What are you doing here, and what are you talking about? Are you insane?"

"Insane with love," breathed Azaza, twining her arms around his neck.

There was more pounding at the door, and a voice shouted, "Your Potency? Are you all right? Why don't you answer? There's a spy loose in the building! Potency?"

"Quite all right, thank you," called the Turtle, trying to disengage himself from Azaza's embrace without being ungentlemanly. "Come in here and explain how a woman got into my quarters."

"We can't get in, your Potency. The door Is barred."

"That's ridiculous. I never lock the door."

"The fact remains, Potency."

"Very well," said the Turtle, "just a moment."

He seized Azaza's wrists, gently but firmly. "Let go this instant!" he whispered fiercely. Azaza obeyed, and the Turtle went to open the door.

"Your Potency," an officer told him excitedly, "it's reported that a woman with strange powers is loose in the BOQ."

"I've met her," said the Turtle grimly, "and some guards I could name have some explaining to do. Send for the Dungeon Officer, and have him bring manacles. Also, bring a torch; I want to see this spy's face in a good light before she's put away."

While the officer ran to summon the Dungeon Officer, the Turtle returned to his sleeping chamber. He found that his mysterious caller was already missing, and so was his sword. His keen mind summed up the situation immediately, and he turned just in time to avoid another murderous blow from Azaza, who was in ambush behind the door. The sword keened past his ear and struck sparks on the floor.

"Are you completely daft?" exclaimed the Turtle irritably, taking the sword away from Azaza again and setting it back on the footlocker. "That's twice now you might have injured me seriously!"

Azaza moaned and sank to the floor, where she lay sobbing bitterly. "I can't help myself," she wept. "I don't want to do it! I love you! I love you passionately, but I'm destined to kill you!"

"I see," said the Turtle doubtfully.

"Save me from myself!" begged Azaza. "Put me in prison, where I can't harm you!"

"There, there," said the Turtle, chivalrously patting her on the head. "A man will be here shortly to take you to a safe place."

A contingent of disheveled officers and worried guards crowded into the room. Several carried lamps or torches. The Dungeon Officer of the day brought a set of manacles. The Turtle indicated Azaza, and the Dungeon Officer stooped to snap the manacles on her wrists. She got up by herself, for no one there had the presence of mind to assist her.

"Has your Potency learned what faction she works for?" asked an officer.

"No," said the Turtle, "and there's no use plying her with questions. She's incoherent—moonstruck. I'm afraid. I doubt that she works for any of our enemies. One thing I do know: when it reaches the point that a poor witless girl can wander into the BOQ and threaten my life, someone isn't doing his job. I invite each of you to examine your conscience tonight because in the morning, it's my turn, and someone will answer for this. Think what havoc a planned infiltration could cause if the Radicals ever find out what kind of security we have in the Central Arsenal. Now, take off that hood, young lady, and let's have a look at you."

Azaza shook the hood off with a toss of her head and turned her tear-stained face for inspection. Several mouths fell open, and someone dropped a torch.

"You!" exclaimed the Turtle." My lo—uh—you tried to kill me," he finished awkwardly.

"We can't lock her up, your Potency," protested the Dungeon Officer, forgetting that the Turtle never changed his mind. "Think what it would do to troop morale. We could never keep order among the dungeon guards."

The Turtle frowned. What to do now? Azaza was the last person in the world he wanted to send to Detention, but he had already committed himself. The Summer Solstice had just passed, and now he could not change his mind and release her until the Winter Solstice, six months hence. The only way to get her out of the dungeon before then would be to file charges and have her brought to trial, which of course, would make things worse. For a moment, he wavered, then his spine stiffened. Duty came first.

"We'll have to lock her up," he said regretfully. "Stealing into the Central Arsenal, at this time of night, is nothing we can simply dismiss."

"Yes, lock me up," breathed Azaza; "keep me where I can't fulfill my destiny! Save me from myself!"

"I'm glad to see you taking it so well," said the Turtle appreciatively.

"Twice tonight, I've failed to kill you," breathed Azaza, "but don't let me try again. Destiny can't blame me for failure, can It?"

"Of course not," said the Turtle. "No one's blaming you. You're obviously not responsible. Now, get a good night's sleep, and perhaps you'll feel better in the morning."

He patted her shoulder consolingly, whereupon Azaza fixed him with a look of such abandoned devotion that he quickly withdrew his hand, embarrassed. He steeled himself and motioned toward the door. The Dungeon Officer led Azaza away, and she looked back adoringly at the Turtle until he was out of view. The Turtle turned to his officers, raised one eyebrow, and shrugged. The officers nodded wisely and filed out of the room.

When things were back to normal, the Turtle lay down again and tried to sleep, but he was much too upset. His beloved was in the dungeon for six weary months, just because he had made his hasty pronouncement before he realized who she was. On top of the tragedy, the mystery: why had she felt she had to kill him when her professed love for him apparently surpassed even his for her? Simple revenge, for his frightful *faux pas* in the Teahouse of the Three Moons, would have made sense. This was something more serious. How unfortunate that the military courts did not recognize mental illness; it would have provided a loophole.

A loophole—where could he find one? And, having found it, how could he make use of it without changing his mind?

In the dungeon below, Azaza lay on a straw pallet, wrapped in her cloak, and felt wonderfully at peace; calmer than she had been at any time since her encounter with the Saint. The scurrying of rats, and the dripping of clammy moisture from the granite walls, were a lullaby of peace and security. Exhausted from her shattering experiences and safe at last from Fate, she drifted off to sleep.

The Turtle, after an hour of wild scheming, became more practical and wondered how often he could visit Azaza in the dungeon before the jailers began to suspect his true feelings. It was so easy to start rumors in the army and so difficult to stop them. Even having her transferred to a more comfortable cell in the Tower of Justice was apt to cause a scandal.

A scandal? The Turtle stopped tossing and stiffened in terror. What a ghastly oversight! The only time to suppress rumors was before they started. He sprang from the bed and dashed out into the corridor.

"Ho guards!" he bellowed at the top of his mighty voice. Two guards clattered into view simultaneously at the intersection of corridors, arriving from opposite directions. They met head-on with a tremendous bashing of armor, staggered for a moment, then recovered and dashed toward the Turtle.

"Summon every officer in the building to the foyer!" roared the Turtle. "Immediately!"

The two soldiers slid to a halt, saluted, and ran back the way they had come. The Turtle returned to his rooms, girded on his sword-belt, donned his helmet, and hastened to the spacious foyer, where the denizens of the BOQ were already gathering. Some of the officers were wearing kilts and helmets and no shirts. Some wore sword-belts over their night-shirts. Some were in underwear. About half were barefooted. A few were fully clothed and armed. All of them looked sleepy and irritated.

Their grumbling ceased instantly as the Turtle strode into the foyer wearing an expression of sinister dedication. He stood and glared at the frightened officers while he waited for stragglers to arrive, then he addressed the assemblage.

"Some of you," he said sternly, "were witness to a certain unfortunate incident which took place in this building tonight. Others may have heard stories, which no doubt were unrecognizably distorted."

He paused dramatically and scowled under his helmet.

"Nobody!" he barked, and everyone jumped. "Nobody outside the BOQ is to hear anything about it! Not so much as a whispered syllable! Any wild rumors that may already be circulating are to be violently suppressed and emphatically contradicted! If anyone here is found to be in any way responsible for propagating malicious gossip, about myself or about the other party involved..." He glowered at the nearest officers and watched them cringe.

"...I'LL BEAT HIM INSENSIBLE WITH MY OWN HANDS!"

His roar vibrated the stone walls and shattered windows. Several officers fainted.

"Dismissed," said the Turtle, and strode from the foyer, his heavy sandals crashing on the mosaic.

With that matter settled, he went back to bed and slept soundly until reveille.

SIXTEEN

THE PATRIARCH

"Repent ye," quavered the Patriarch of Kalopolis at the empty library," for the Cataclysm is at hand!" Melli materialized with a soft whir.

"No, no," said the Patriarch. "I wasn't calling you. Just talking to myself. Heh! Talking to myself. Melli, it's come to that. Sometimes I even argue."

Melli darted to the liquor cabinet and brought back the goblet and a flask of the Patriarch's favorite. The old man raised a trembling hand negatively.

"No," he piped firmly, "lead me not into temptation, bless your heart. I feel even worse than I look, but I've got work to do, and I can't concentrate when I'm sozzled."

He dismally scanned the book-laden table. His eyes were red-rimmed and sunken. "The facts I need are somewhere in the Scripture, a few minnows in a sea of information.

If only we had a terse, compact Scripture like the heathen cults. I wouldn't have such a jot, but the sacred literature of the Established Faith is enough to choke a brontosaur."

He removed his skullcap and massaged his pate tenderly, for a headache raged within.

"The Book of Aphorisms alone is in sixteen volumes. Sixteen volumes, mind you, devoted entirely to wise little jingles and bromides that the test of time has proven. The Book of Liturgy is in six volumes. I had to commit all six to memory. I might add, to get my degree in divinity. The Book of Scribes has seventy-three volumes; I guess it takes first prize. Today I'm working on the Book of Prophesy, in thirty-six volumes. I went through fourteen of them just today—scanning, of course. Ironically, all I've learned so far is that my latest scheme was another flop."

Melli seemed only mildly surprised.

"It failed," grieved the Patriarch, "just as miserably as all the others. I was up all night working it out, and a fine piece of engineering it was, but I miscalculated somewhere. You remember, ten days ago. I sent you to the Capital to drop an old sandal on that coppersmith's trash-heap?"

Melli nodded.

"From several references in the Scripture. I'd figured out what I thought was the exact day and hour Azaza was to make her destined attempt on the Turtle's life. I only had a few days to stop her; otherwise, I'd never have risked planting an anomaly that close to the Temple of the Macrocosm. Fortunately, we got away with it. An alley cat was destined to start yowling that night, and he, at least, came through in good form. The coppersmith's wife, half asleep, came stumbling out into the alley, found the sandal where you planted it, and threw it at the cat. It missed the cat and went through the window of a printing shop next door, where it smashed an inkwell. The printer had been hired to circulate invitations to an informal luncheon scheduled for the day before yesterday, and the spilled ink obliterated part of the list of guests. The printer managed to figure out all the smudged names except one, that of a certain countess, who happened to have commissioned a struggling young artist to do her portrait. The artist had a date with Azaza, but he needed five crowns more cash than he had. His patroness, whose invitation to the luncheon hadn't been delivered because of the ink, was in a vile temper over what she imagined was a snub, so she took it out on the artist by refusing an advance he asked for. I watched the whole sequence, and up to that point, everything went perfectly. Next, according to my calculations, the painter was supposed to show up at Azaza's house, five crowns light of the usual fee, and be summarily rebuffed since Azaza's trying to weed his type out of her clientele. He was supposed to brood over this for a while, then try to get even—and I had this particular reaction calculated to nearly eighty-five percent probability—by denouncing Azaza for aiding and abetting revolutionaries. The charge wouldn't have stuck, but Azaza couldn't assassinate the Turtle if she was in jail on suspicion at the moment. I figured she was destined to try it."

The Patriarch moaned softly. "So what happens? The artist got to Azaza's house and was informed that she was already under arrest for attempted assassination! One sequence of events—the anomaly—I had figured to a fine hair, but the other sequence—that I thought was destined-developed a cumulative error of nearly thirty-six hours! Figure that one out!"

Melli set down the flask and the goblet. The Patriarch stared at them longingly but held himself in check with the iron self-discipline leftover from his sainthood.

"So now I've got to start all over," he said despondently. "But I'll hit it yet. I've found some more leads in the Scripture. Half a dozen prophets make passing reference to this Cataclysm. Maybe today, with the will of All There Is, I'll find a more thorough discussion of it. I've got to have facts—gospel facts. My own calculations are too inexact, and we've seen what happens when I try to rely on them. By the way. I hope these errands all over the Empire aren't too tiring?"

Melli made a deprecatory gesture.

"You're a jewel. Melli. You're the only one I can count on, any more. Even the Prime Ecclesiarch's reconciled to the destruction of the Church. Well. I'll find the answer one of these days. Unless I get a case of the shakes first, better leave that flask handy, just in case. I won't touch it, of course, unless I start seeing things that are neither material nor spiritual."

He turned reluctantly back to his reading—the Book of Prophesy, Volume XV, Part one, Chapter Four, Verse 778.

"If only the Church's fate didn't all depend on one pour old sinner," he whined, "but it's all up to me, and I can't shirk my responsibility. No one else cares. I've checked on every saint in the Empire, and they're all busily verifying the prophecy. You'd think at least the Prime Ecclesiarch would have enough guts to do something, but the old slob won't lift a finger. Too fat to fight, and too holy to give a damn."

The Patriarch leaned back in his chair and rubbed his eyes. "Seventeen volumes to go. Melli, and that's only the Book of Prophesy, and if I don't find enough by scanning. I'll have to go through it all again more carefully. Already I've got a rip-snorter of a headache. I'll never give up, though—never! My disciple, waltzing around the Capital messing up people's lives, thinks I'm a harmless old fool, but he's in for the shock of his life; I swear it! There's a lot of spirituality left in these bones!"

He shook his talon-like fist at the ceiling. "My mortal will against the Plan of Destiny doesn't look like anything to lay odds on," he piped fiercely, "but I'm due for my second wind. When the Patriarch of Kalopolis gets his hackles up, the Universe had better get up pretty damned early in the morning!"

SEVENTEEN

THE TURTLE

The soldier's Adam's apple moved up, then down. He was trying to stand at attention but was trembling so badly he could scarcely make himself heard above the jangle of his armor.

"I don't know how it ever got out, Potency," he squeaked, "but it's all over town."

The Turtle was on the brink of apoplexy. "Do you mean to stand there," he roared, "and tell me that people would <u>dare</u> say such things?"

"Well, your Potency. I mean, there was Azaza, and there you were, and well, I mean the obvious inference. I mean obvious to a soldier's mind, well naturally the facts are something else again, but you know how rumors get started and well, gee whiz, your Potency, after all, most unmarried officers would literally <u>bask</u> in this sort of thing."

"Oh my stars," groaned the Turtle, wrapping his head in his hands. "Oh my heavens, Oh my reputation. By the way, how is it that a mere corporal was sent to report this calamity?"

"Well, Potency, as I understand it, the major general in charge of rumor control was kind of reluctant to tell you himself, so he sent a brigadier general, who sent a colonel, and so on, and finally it got down to me, and I couldn't find a private."

The Turtle was past the crisis now and going safely into shock. The soldier resumed breathing.

"Oh, great, Zas," moaned the Turtle. "What to do now?

Actually, there's only one course open to me: I'll have to go into hiding. When this scandal blows over, I'll take an assumed name, grow a mustache, and apply for my command again. I hope it's not too late, by then, to save the Empire. Incidentally, you may stand at ease. I'm sorry I kept you at attention so long. I'm not thinking very clearly. Hearing about this scandal has really given me a start. It surpasses my worst fears."

"If I may be so bold as to call something to your Potency's attention," the soldier said timorously, "it's your Potency's very presence here in the Arsenal that's keeping the wrong-thinkers underground. If your Potency abandons the army at a time like this, the Empire's a gone goose. The Radicals, especially, will be up in arms before you can say Long Live His Radiance."

"I know. I know," said the Turtle sadly, "but I just can't face it. Our enemies have found my Achilles' tendon. When I pass through the streets, the people will whisper. When I attend the imperial court, all the ladies will be giggling behind their fans. I can't face it."

"Courage, your Potency," urged the soldier. "Just giggle right back at them, if you know what I mean."

"No, my good man, it's not a matter of courage at all. Since I was old enough for my first toy sword, I've never flinched in the face of danger, but against the cowardly invisible arrows of gossip, no shield will avail me. My only recourse is to leave town, now, within the hour. Fortunately, I happen to have a disguise ready."

The Turtle crossed the room to the closet, took out his duffle-bag, and rummaged through it till he found a monkish brown robe and hood.

"I've kept this for just such an emergency," he explained." No one will recognize me in this. Let that be a lesson to you: a real soldier is always ready for anything, anything at all. My motto is: Be Prepared."

He removed his helmet, slipped into the habit, and pulled up the hood. He went to the mirror to practice looking holy.

"Your Potency?" said the soldier.

"What is it, my good man?"

"Your Potency, what shall I tell—well—anyone who might ask me?"

"Tell the truth," counseled the Turtle. "You'll never go wrong telling the truth, even if only for its own sake. If everyone believed that. I wouldn't be in this fix."

"Very well, your Potency."

"You're excused," said the Turtle," and spare yourself the trouble of saluting on your way out. I've just resigned my commission."

The soldier ran to report the terrible news. The Turtle wrote out his resignation, carefully explaining why it was in the Empire's best interests, and left it on his desk. He packed a few essentials and left the Central Arsenal by a postern gate.

EIGHTEEN

THE SCARECROW

The Scarecrow worked frantically to finish the Figure within the prescribed five days. After the Saint left him, he worked all night till dawn, then all day till dusk, and so on for five nights and days. Hunger gnawed his ribs, and sleeplessness blurred his vision, but he could not stop. His compulsion-driven hands shook and fumbled, spilling acids and molten metals. Sometimes he burned himself, but never seriously enough to stop his work.

Miraculously, and to the Scarecrow's bitter exasperation, none of these many accidents touched the Figure itself. The device was constructed of hundreds of interacting parts, each one cast from a precisely-blended alloy of rare metals. There were a thousand places where he could have made a slight error and rendered it harmless, but even the few deliberate mistakes he managed to make were canceled out by genuine mistakes. The Scarecrow came to hate this invention more viciously than he had ever hated anything, which is saying a great deal, but it took shape swiftly and surely, and it became increasingly apparent that the project, which should have taken weeks, would be finished before the deadline with a few hours to spare.

Tearfully he broke the components from their individual molds, tempered them, verified their dimensions and properties, and soldered them in place. At intervals, he screamed imprecations on everyone in the building whose name he could remember, hoping desperately that someone would be annoyed enough to come in and kill him. It did no good. The tenants had all been driven to using earplugs or moving out. The landlady had left her husband and was staying with relatives in another town. The landlord himself was under restraint by Destiny; the Saint had apologetically forbidden him to interfere with the Scarecrow in any way.

In the late afternoon of the fifth day, the Scarecrow soldered the last element in place, hurled the soldering iron through the last pane of glass in the window, and collapsed into a chair. The finished masterpiece of alchemistic engineering sat on the table and seemed to sneer at him. The Scarecrow glared at it, hating it for what it would do in the Neutrals' hands. He wondered blackly how soon his enemies would come for it.

It occurred to him then that for the first time in several days, he was moving of his own volition, instead of in rebellious obedience to compulsion. He looked at his hands and moved them experimentally to make certain. With a triumphant yell, he sprang to his feet, seized a hatchet, turned on the Figure...and froze.

His free agency left off at that point. He could not destroy his invention.

Nor would he give up trying while he had any latitude at all. He paced back and forth, giving the Figure sidelong glances, then tried again to smash it. He froze.

He threw the useless hatchet at a cluster of bottles. They smashed, spilling chemicals, which promptly dissolved a hole in the table and dribbled through to eat at the floor. The Scarecrow approached the Figure as calmly as his furious hatred would allow and picked it up. Nothing stopped him. He carried it to an open window and looked out. Three stories below was a paved courtyard. Moving suddenly, in an effort to take Destiny unawares, he tried to throw the Figure out to be smashed beyond repair on the stones, but his muscles would not respond to his will.

He set the Figure down and went to find an empty coal sack. He wrapped the Figure in the sack, lifted it to his shoulder, and started for the door. Everything went smoothly. He hurried down the back stairs to the ground floor and out into the late afternoon sunlight.

So far, so good; but what next? The Saint had warned him he

could not escape, but if the Plan of Destiny required split-second timing, perhaps even eluding the Neutrals until sometime after sundown would cause enough confusion to make their party's ultimate supremacy less than inevitable. He could lose nothing by trying. The problem was to choose a hiding place that had not been destined. Perhaps he could bury the prize and cause a delay while the Neutrals dug up the neighborhood in search of it.

He sneaked away from the house, across the road, and into a clump of bushes. The only tool he found was a sharp stick. The ground was hard, and he ran into rocks a few inches below the surface. His stick broke. He controlled his temper, hefted the sack, and ran awkwardly across a plowed field, keeping next to a hedgerow for concealment. He crossed another road and another field and came to the river. It was broad and placid at this point, sparkling in the sunlight as it drifted southward toward Kalopolis.

The Scarecrow walked to the water's edge, hitched up his robe, waded out into the stream until the water was up to his thighs, took the Figure from his shoulder, and, of course, froze.

Cursing savagely, he put the oppressive load back on his shoulder and waded to shore. It was no use. He could go where he pleased and do as he pleased as long as he did not try to destroy the Figure. Probably, he thought, Destiny would let him drop the Figure on a trash heap and leave it if he wished, but if he did, some Neutral would certainly happen by and find it.

Only a man with vast reserves of stubbornness could have weathered all the Scarecrow's years of relentlessly consistent misfortune, but he was finally weakening. Who could deny, by this time, that the Neutrals were Destiny's Chosen Party? However much he despised them, he was only a mortal. For a moment, he was tempted to give up and abandon the secret weapon to its fate, but then he thought of its awful powers. As soon as the Neutrals captured it, it would automatically adjust itself and begin winning universal adulation for its new owners, and it was only a matter of time before he himself, its inventor, would have fallen victim to its powers and would be happily and willingly serving the Neutrals' villainous ends. The thought was unbearable. The fifth day was not over yet; he still had till sundown.

He looked around. Up by the next bend of the river stood the cottage where the ferryman stayed. There was nothing beyond the river but farms, and so few people ever passed that way that neither the township nor the province had ever bothered to build a bridge. The ferryman lived by the river, and when someone came by and wanted to cross, he worked. The rest of the time, he sat around in front of his cottage, when the weather permitted, trailed a fishing line, and played his ocarina. The strains of a country tune drifted from that direction now.

If the Scarecrow could not drown the Figure himself, perhaps someone else could. If the ferryman refused to cooperate, then one glimpse of the Figure would instantly win him over. The Scarecrow stilled the misgivings that welled up in the back of his mind and trudged upstream to call on the ferryman. The ferryman, a hale and chunky rube with twinkling eyes and a wind-burned face was noted for his neighborliness, and the Scarecrow doubted that he would have to use the Figure's persuasive powers, which he had come to regard as obscene.

"Hey," the ferryman greeted cheerily, as the Scarecrow came up, "leaving town?"

"No," said the Scarecrow. "Not exactly. Not now."

"What's up then?" The ferryman pointed his ocarina at the far bank of the river. "Want to cross?" he asked hopefully.

"No. I have a favor to ask of you," said the Scarecrow. "It's terribly important."

"Gladly," said the ferryman. "Just name it." · "This," said the Scarecrow, indicating his burden, "is dangerous, and I can't get rid of it. Could you throw it in the river for me?"

"I guess so," said the ferryman, "but why don't you do it yourself, so you'll know the job's done right? Take my skiff, if you want. No charge, unless whatever it is blows up and sinks the skiff."

"That's not the danger," said the Scarecrow, "And I can't do it myself. I've tried, and I can't. There are...sentimental attachments."

"I guess it's none of my business, but you've sort of got my curiosity up. What is it?"

"There's no time to explain. I'm an alchemist, and I've created something I'm afraid of. Please don't ask any more questions about it, and please don't look at it. Just take it out to the deepest water and throw it in. I'll pay you as well as I can."

At the mention of alchemy, the ferryman's eyes narrowed slightly." I see," he said. "Well, it sounds fishy to me, but times are hard, and I reckon there's no sense in passing up an honest copper."

"A copper? I'll give you a crown! And I swear it won't hurt you as long as you restrain your curiosity and don't open the sack."

"You have the face of an honest man," said the ferryman, "so I won't question your word. Put it in the skiff while I fetch a pair of oars."

When the bundle was perched on the stern where the ferryman could conveniently kick it overboard, the Scarecrow helped him launch the boat. He offered to pay for the errand in advance. The ferryman shook his head. He pulled at the oars and drew away from the shore.

"No," he said cheerfully," I can't take your money. I'll get rid of this thing for you, but not exactly the way you had in mind. These are hard times, and we can't afford to just dump things in the river."

"You don't know what you're saying! I tell you that sack is dangerous!"

"Don't give it another thought, neighbor. I'll take care of everything."

The doubts lurking in the Scarecrow's mind congealed into horrified certainty. He splashed out into the water after the retreating rowboat, but the soft mud mired his feet and slowed him. The ferryman escaped by a considerable margin and turned downstream.

"Throw it in!" the Scarecrow pleaded frantically. "You must! It's imperative! Where are you going?"

"To Kalopolis," came the light-hearted reply. "A holy man dropped by a couple days back and warned me you'd be along, but I didn't know who he was talking about till you mentioned alchemy. Your invention's in good hands. Don't worry about a thing."

"You're a Neutral!" screamed the Scarecrow. "Come back, you thieving jackal!"

The boat was already in deep water, and the Scarecrow could not swim.

"If there's any way I can ever return this favor," called the ferryman, "be sure to look me up."

The Scarecrow stood helplessly, up to his knees in water, and watched the boat, the Figure, and the ferryman dwindle into the distance, aided by the current and moving much more swiftly than he could have run along the bank. He watched until the boat rounded a bend and disappeared.

The sun, he noticed, was just setting.

Dazed with grief, he waded back to shore. In the ferryman's cottage, he opened all the windows, overturned a can of turpentine, and set it alight. He was far from content with this token revenge, but it was all he could do.

At some moment, while he was watching the flames spread, he gave an involuntary mental shrug and dropped all the burdens of his life by the wayside. When he turned away from the blazing cottage, he was completely transformed. His jaw hung slack. His eyes, no longer wild, were dull and vacuous. He stared vapidly back at the conflagration, failing to comprehend it. His volatile emotions were finally calmed and replaced with a limp, sickly peace of mind. He stumbled away up the riverbank toward the woods, and for many weeks after that, he remembered nothing.

NINETEEN

THE SAINT AND THE TURTLE

On his way back from the South, the Saint stopped at several points along the road to attend to details of the world's destiny. When these were out of the way, he paused to scan the immediate future and saw it was time to arrange for the next phase of the Turtle's career. He continued north for a while and paused when he came within half a day's journey of the Capital.

"This is the best place to wait for him," he mused. "He will be in just the right frame of mind when he reaches this point."

Accordingly, he stepped off the road to stand by a large tree. As he waited, he looked around at the peaceful, idyllic countryside. A flock of crows raided a nearby field and were driven off by small boys throwing jagged stones. A snake swallowed a field mouse. A cat killed a bird, and ten minutes later was itself run over by a passing carriage. The passenger in the carriage, the Saint happened to notice, was a young nobleman who was destined to be poisoned the next day by his betrothed. Since it had nothing to do with his own mission, the Saint refrained from thinking about the circum-stances of the impending tragedy.

"How irrational all this would seem to a careless observer," he reflected, "and yet how perfectly it all functions, if one knows the Truth. How stifled is the outlook of the layman, to whom the all-pervading poetry of Destiny's Plan seems merely random movement—an intricate machine of unknown function, a treatise in an unknown tongue."

He looked up to watch the Turtle approach, exactly on schedule, staring morosely at the road before him. He walked very slowly, and the imaginary snare-drums, throbbing at funeral tempo, were subliminally faint. The brown robe was not a bad disguise, all in all, except that it was a little too short for him, and a suspicious observer might have noticed he was still wearing steel greaves and army sandals.

The Saint stepped out onto the road. "Peace be with you, my son," he greeted.

"Well, father," said the Turtle, "imagine meeting you here. Come to think of it, though, you did say we'd meet again, didn't you?"

"It was destined," said the Saint.

"I'm glad to see you," said the Turtle, "There has been quite a load on my mind, and I'm sorely in need of some spiritual counsel if I wouldn't be imposing on your time,"

"It is no imposition, my son. That is why I met you here."

"Oh, is it? How did you know?"

The Saint smiled slightly and spread his hands.

"Well," said the Turtle, "I suppose real holy men know all sorts of things. Speaking of holy men. I hope you won't be annoyed by this disguise. There's been some scandal, you see, and I wanted to leave the Capital incognito."

"I know," said the Saint kindly, "and you have my entire sympathy. The purest love is often the target of the most thoughtless gossip. In this case. I should advise you to forget about her for the time being."

"Forget about her?"

"Yes, forget her completely."

"Forget whom? I don't understand."

"No matter," said the Saint.

"You have other things on your mind. Perhaps I can be of some help."

"Thank you, father. I appreciate having a sympathetic listener at a time like this. You see, the Opposition, among others, was threatening armed revolt when I left, and I feel rather guilty about leaving when I did, though I do think there were extenuating circumstances."

"Of course there were," the Saint soothed. "It was entirely beyond your control, and you ought not to blame yourself. Please forget the Opposition."

"I suppose you're right; it couldn't be helped. I'll take your advice and forget...whatever it was. Yet I'm afraid his Imperial Radiance was more or less counting on me."

"His Imperial Radiance is beyond all anxiety," said the Saint, bowing his head. "Long live his Radiance."

"What? Do you mean...?"

"Yes, my son; the Emperor's heart failed him when he learned of your resignation, but of course, it was no fault of yours."

"This is terrible," gasped the Turtle. "What a time for me to be missing! I'm needed back at the Capital! Besides. I should be there for the reading of the imperial will. I have some reason to believe that I may have been...er...mentioned."

"Yes, you are the Emperor's sole heir."

"Great Zas! I must get back to the Capital with all deliberate speed!"

"No, my son," corrected the Saint, "you must forget the Capital and everything in the Capital."

"What Capital, father?"

The conversation went on in this vein for some time, and as they talked of one thing and another, the Turtle's worried brow grew more and more serene.

"I must not keep you from your travels any longer," the Saint said at last, "if you are to reach the next hamlet by nightfall. I do hope I have managed to ease your mind a little."

"Indeed you have," said the Turtle gratefully. "My petty troubles don't seem nearly so important to me now as they did half an hour ago. Come to think of it. I don't recall what was bothering me. Isn't it amazing how a little intelligent conversation with someone else helps us to see things from their normal perspective? I'm sorry to have taken up your time with anything so trivial. How can I thank you?"

"Do not thank me, for this conversation was as much a part of my destiny as it was of yours and has been predestined from the beginning of time."

"But it's also predestined that I express my appreciation," said the Turtle wittily, "so thanks again."

"Go in peace, my son," said the Saint, gesturing his parting benediction. "We shall meet again."

"Soon. I hope," said the Turtle.

With a touch of melancholy, the Saint watched the Turtle set out in the general direction of Kalopolis, trying to remember who he was and where he was going. There were no snare-drums at all, now.

"It seems unfortunate," the Saint murmured, "that such a promising career must be interrupted, but the ways of the Universe are not our ways, and we may not presume to pass moral judgment on All There Is. Besides, he will also make a passable holy man."

For the first few days, Azaza's love for the Turtle and the knowledge that she was in prison for his safety shielded her more than adequately from the discomforts of the dungeon. She rejoiced that she was safe from her compulsion, that her attempt to fulfill the prophecy had failed, and that if she could not be with the Turtle, at least she could be near him, for the dungeon—by some ancient architect's whim or error—was directly underneath the BOQ.

As the days passed, however, and the pastel clouds in which she floated began to wear thin, she took more critical notice of her surroundings. Despite the heat of summer, it was always clammy and chilly that far underground. The bedding was hardly what she was used to; in fact, she suspected that several prisoners had slept on the heap of straw since it had last been changed. The food for the prisoners was procured with an eye to the imperial budget and was so coarse that Azaza passed up several meals before she was hungry enough to stomach it. She was annoyed and depressed by the continual moaning and occasional screams from nearby cells. The bare, rough-cut granite motif of the interior decoration did not long remain an interesting novelty. The list of Azaza's complaints expanded every day, and when the days had fused into weeks, and she was losing count of the weeks, she finally admitted to herself that her glee at being in the dungeon was becoming rather forced.

Was it possible, she wondered, that the Turtle was still indifferent toward her even after meeting her twice so that her sacrifice was unappreciated? Or was it possible that the prophecy had already been fulfilled in some unexpected manner? These doubts and a hundred others paraded through her mind as she languished in Detention, and the theme was always the same: Was there or was there not a worthwhile purpose in staying where she was? Because, unless her imprisonment was necessary for her beloved's safety, she would rather leave. The fact that she was three stories below street level, surrounded by impassable bedrock, and barred from daylight—not to mention freedom—by several cast-iron doors and an indeterminate number of armed guards was beside the point. All the dungeon guards were men, and under all but the most extraordinary circumstances, men did what Azaza wanted. The question of escaping or not escaping was solely one of conscience. The decision was made very difficult, however, by her present insulation from current events. For Azaza's own protection (as the authorities had put it), the guards were forbidden to talk to her.

One day, which might have been one night for all she knew, as Azaza lay on her straw pallet trying to sleep, a shadow fell across the small, barred window in the cell's massive door. Azaza glanced up and saw that it was just the Dungeon Officer. She closed her eyes again, disdainfully. The Dungeon Officer was never the same man twice, for it was unpopular duty and rotated every day. The shadow did not go away immediately, and Azaza opened her eyes for another look. The officer, flagrantly disregarding regulations, had tarried by the grill and was leering at her.

"Hi handsome," she greeted.

The head glanced furtively in both directions. "Ehh!" said the officer sternly. "Do you want to get me in trouble? You know it's against regulations for us to talk together."

He moved away, and Azaza heard his footsteps retreating down the corridor, pausing by various cells to see if anyone had escaped recently. Azaza listened, and after a while, the officer's tour of inspection was diverted in her direction again, as such tours always were. This officer impressed Azaza as more reasonable than most; it might be a chance to get some news. Resolving to try a little harder than usual, Azaza got up, threw her cloak aside, and quickly straightened her hair, and smoothed her dress as well as she could on short notice. There was little she could do under the circumstances to make herself beautiful, but most of her beauty was her own, so little preening was necessary. When the officer paused by the grill to leer at her again, she was ready for him.

"Hello," she said, whispering this time.

The officer frowned and looked up and down the corridor. No one was spying on him. He hesitated, then looked in at the grill again, and smiled stupidly. Azaza drew close to the door to facilitate conversation.

"Why isn't anyone allowed to talk to me?" she asked wistfully.

"It's against regulations," replied the officer promptly, as if this were reason enough, "Besides," he added, "it would raise hell with morale. If we didn't keep the guards under the strictest restraint concerning lady prisoners, they'd be dueling each other for the privilege of dungeon duty. If the guards were allowed to talk to you, they'd be tempted to violate other regulations, and it could lead to considerable embarrassment for you, as well as us."

"It gets awfully lonely," said Azaza.

"I guess it does," said the officer sympathetically.

"You don't know how nice it is to have someone to talk to, for a change," said Azaza sweetly, "especially a handsome captain."

"Aw, shucks," said the officer, who was only a first lieutenant.

"Captain, how long will it be before I'm brought to trial?"

"Well. I guess it might be quite a spell. His Potency will have to bring charges against you, so I guess you're sort of stuck here till he turns up."

"Turns up?" Azaza echoed. "What do you mean?"

"Well. I guess you know he disappeared."

"The Turtle disappeared? When? Where did he go?"

"Shh! Not so loud. Whisper. I'm supposed to set an example for the troops, and if anyone thinks I'm talking with you, it'll be bad for morale...His Potency resigned his command and vanished into thin air about a week ago, I guess. Nobody knows where he is. We tried to keep it a military secret, but then his Radiance died, and it turned out the Turtle was successor to the throne. We finally had to admit he was gone. There's been nothing but trouble ever since— one long riot. I guess his Potency was the only one the Radicals were afraid of. Excuse me; I hear someone coming. I might be back."

The officer walked away, trying to look nonchalant. So her beloved Turtle had resigned his command and left her in Detention, had he? Azaza immediately suppressed her twinge of annoyance. The Turtle undoubtedly had good reasons for his actions, and she would not question them. However, if the army could not find him, it did not seem likely that she could either, so there was no danger in leaving the dungeon. And, was not the mere fact of the Turtle's resignation sufficient proof that the prophecy was fulfilled? This obsession with killing him had all been a foolish misunderstanding on her part. Of course, Destiny would not be so cruel as to force her actually to kill the man she loved.

The Dungeon Officer did, in fact, find time to come back. Azaza stood a few inches away from the door so that more of her figure would be visible through the small grill.

"Hello, handsome," she breathed. "I missed you terribly."

"Well, heh, heh," replied the officer with a broad grin, "I sure missed you, too. I guess."

"You're in charge of this floor, aren't you, Captain?" asked Azaza in admiring tones.

"Well, um, yes; as a matter of fact, I'm in charge of the whole dungeon," boasted the officer, "at least for today."

"Captain," sighed Azaza, "I've been in this nasty old cell for just weeks and weeks. Don't you think I could walk around in the corridors for a little while, just to stretch my legs?"

"Oh God no!" said the officer, blenching. "It would be against regulations, and think what it would do with troop morale if anybody ever found out!"

"You're fascinating to talk to, captain," said Azaza, "and you have such a nice voice, even when you whisper."

"Why, shucks, thank you," said the Dungeon Officer, grinning again.

Azaza batted her eyelids seductively. "I'd love to get to know you better.

"Well—uh—yes, it's sure too bad. I guess, that—well—"

"Captain," whispered Azaza passionately, "after all, you are in charge here, and this nasty old door is coming between us." She watched the officer's confusion through artfully drooping eyelashes. "Between you..." she murmured sexily, "...and me.

"Well—I guess maybe—hmm—oh well; You only live once. Just a minute; I'll get the keys."

Escaping from a dungeon is never a facile operation. Having

gulled and ditched the officer (who dared not sound the alarm), Azaza had to knock out one guard, compromise with four others, and make innumerable false promises, but as such things go, her escape was reasonably easy. After a couple of hours and a number of vicissitudes, she reached the BOQ by way of the cellar stairs. Hearing footsteps approaching from around a corner, she opened a door at random and glided inside. The footsteps passed harmlessly by, and Azaza found herself in an officer's bedroom, alone with a sleeping officer. He was probably on duty at night.

She improvised rapidly. There was no make-up on her face after all the time she had been in the dungeon, so she was off to a good start. She took off her cloak, folded it, and wound it around her torso to modify her unsoldierly contours, then found the officer's armor and buckled it on. She piled her hair on top of her head and covered it with his helmet. She buckled on his sword belt, slipped her legs into his greaves, laced his oversized, iron-cleated sandals on her feet, and left the room without waking him. Staggering under the weight, she left the BOQ and set out for the main gate.

Her disguise was far from perfect. Her walk, for one thing, was the result of lifelong habit, and it did not occur to her that a real soldier who swayed his hips so seductively was certain to attract unfavorable attention. For another thing, her hands, arms, knees, and face were visible, and none of these features went well with the armor. Everyone she passed stopped to stare suspiciously. Whatever they thought of this effeminate officer, they all assumed there was dirty work afoot, which was none of their business, and Azaza passed through the main gate to freedom.

Her real troubles began after she had discarded the armor in an alley and returned to her own house. The Conservative forces were still in control of the city, but their hold was precarious, and localized outbreaks of rioting and looting had become so frequent they were almost a bore to everyone not directly affected. Azaza received her first tangible evidence of the current political situation when she found her house stripped of everything salable and her servants deserted *en masse*, probably to join the looters when they moved on to the next house. The loss of her furniture did not matter, for she would have had to abandon it anyway to get out of town quickly and inconspicuously, but she had hoped at least to pick up some fresh clothes and some money and valuables. The looters had not even left her enough for coach fare. Her sole remaining possessions were the clothes she was wearing. She did not even have a pair of sandals, for she had had to abandon hers when she donned the officer's military clogs.

There was nothing to do but make the best of things, and she knew that whatever she did had better be done somewhere else. The Imperial Capital, infested with Conservative police, was a poor place for an escaped political prisoner to start a new life.

Azaza fashioned some sandals out of straw and quitted the city on foot, heading south. She fell in with a caravan of travelers bound for Kalopolis. The barbarians, they reported, had invaded the northern provinces and were sweeping south. The Imperial Regulars could not march north to oppose them, for the move would have left the Radicals a clear field. Until the future of the Empire was a little more certain, these good people felt that the South was a safer place. Azaza joined the refugees and rapidly built up a clientele among them.

She did not go all the way to Kalopolis. As an escapee from the Central Arsenal, she would be wanted by police in every major city of the Empire. When she had saved up several hundred crowns, she stopped in a small town a few leagues north of Kalopolis, where there was no Regular Army garrison. There she rented a house, advertised for servants, hung out her shingle, and immediately prospered.

TWENTY

THE EMPEROR AND THE SAINT

The Emperor had been presiding as usual over the Hall of Kings when the Turtle's resignation was brought to him. He had contemplated the appalling news only for a moment, then had fallen into a swoon from which he very wisely never recovered.

The sudden and dramatic death of a head of state was difficult to keep secret, but officialdom had better luck in concealing the Turtle's disappearance, so it was several weeks before the plunge into total chaos. Riots went on as before, but with a certain reserve. The imperial last will and testament designated the Turtle as sole beneficiary and heir to the throne, and the commoners' previous contests with the Turtle had left a lasting impression. The forty-one heirs-apparent also had reason to hesitate, for although their grateful admiration for the Turtle turned abruptly to wrathful contempt, and proceedings began at once to have the Emperor's will declared illegal, invalid, and insane, the kings were unwilling to resort to violence until they were sure the Supreme Tribunal would fail them.

The last rites for his Imperial Radiance were performed by the Prime Ecclesiarch of the Established Faith, and the ceremony embodied all the pomp and pageantry that Church and State could devise. The extravaganza was three weeks in preparation and went perfectly except for one flaw: The Emperor's heir was glaringly, flagrantly, egregiously not present. A leak here and a leak there had already started rumors which were now obviously substantiated, and the commoners reacted lustily. During the obsequies, the Prime Ecclesiarch had to raise his hoarse voice to be heard above the tumult outside the Citadel wall, where the Radicals were exuberantly demonstrating against the government and distributing arms to the rabble.

By the time the Emperor's last remains had been deposited with those of his forebears, there were no more illusions. The Imperial Regulars withdrew amid a cloudburst of spears and arrows. The Citadel portcullises slammed, the drawbridges rose, archers swarmed to the battlements, and the Revolution was on. The Radicals, unopposed, took over the rest of the city.

Responsibility for naming a provisional Emperor devolved upon the Hall of Kings, which reconvened in extraordinary session for the purpose. As each delegate valuably promoted the favorite-son pretender from his own province, the pretenders themselves marshaled their troops and hurried to the Capital to support their respective delegates. The Radicals' assault on the Imperial Citadel was interrupted by the arrival of a provincial army. The king who led it fought through the Radical encirclement and presented his claim before the Hall of Kings. It was, of course, rejected by a vote of forty to one. After the thwarted pretender had driven off a Radical counterattack and had had it out with another ambitious monarch who arrived just then, he laid siege to the Citadel himself, until word arrived that local insurgents had seized his provincial capital. He and his troops marched off to restore order, and the Radicals renewed their assault until the next pretender arrived.

Time passed, summer relapsed into autumn, and the strife spread rapidly into every province. In the North, the Imperial Regulars' undermanned outposts crumpled before the long-awaited onslaught, and the barbarians swept down from their frozen wilderness to ravage the countryside. In the Midlands, every conceivable faction came into the open to stage successful but impermanent coups against the Conservatives and against each other. In the South, where the reformist spirit was not so strong among the commoners, it was the royalty and nobility who took advantage of the confusion to go to war among themselves over coveted real estate and old grudges.

Amid all this, the central government swayed and tottered but miraculously stood. According to the Great Charter, each province was to appoint its own delegate to the Hall of Kings, subject to the Emperor's veto. Normally these delegates were of royal blood. They wore crowns, held the title of Majesty, and were empowered to make binding agreements on behalf of the brothers, uncles, or cousins whom they represented. Now, as provinces changed hands, the insurgents sent delegates of their own. At first, this was only a gesture of protest, but it was unexpectedly successful, for there was no Emperor to challenge the newcomers. The Great Charter was examined carefully, but there were no loopholes, and the imposters had to be sworn in. When revolutionists of all classes learned of this, they abandoned their plans to take the Imperial Capital and fought instead for control of individual provinces and representation in the Hall of Kings. No party could hope to control more than one province at a time, but they all felt that one would be enough. Each new delegate arrived with the conviction that as soon as he outlined his own new concept of government, the compellingly self-evident validity of his party's ideology would take the Hall by storm.

The Hall filled up with lean, disorderly Radicals in work clothes, shifty-eyed Neutrals in brocaded vests, trim, athletic Vegetarians in Lincoln green, and assorted picturesque delegates representing small, regional parties—outlaw bands in some cases—who had won tentative primacy in their own provinces. The bandit chieftains wore leather shirts and coonskin caps. There were two graybeards in brown cassocks from backward southern provinces where a cabal of heretic priests had set up a theocracy. As the tides of battle turned, youthful, wondering delegates were sent by resurgent Conservative governments, which had lost most of their mature royalty in warfare and had to be represented in the Capital by very young crown princes. The only competent representatives left were from the far North, where barbarians had invaded before there was time for a decisive revolution. Since no barbarian delegates came to claim their seats, the original proxies remained, hoping unrealistically for better days ahead.

Although technically the central government still stood, the Old Order as a living reality was reduced to a small and dwindling remnant. There was the handful of exiled bonafide kings in the

Hall. There was the framework of imperial government, which was currently useless but not necessarily meaningless. There were a few companies of soldiers in the Imperial Citadel, who at least served the very useful purpose of preventing the more fanatic representatives from bringing weapons into the Hall. There were a few scattered castles, where stubborn knights and their retainers were making a firm stand against besieging partisans.

As the Secretary Royal expected, the coalition government accomplished nothing. So varied were the delegates in ideals and in temperaments that they could not agree on so much as the Rules of Order, which, as a matter of principle, most of them wanted to revise. They made the best of it and did without rules. Enacting laws or choosing a successor to the deceased Emperor was beyond reasonable hope. It did not matter, really, for the provincial governments were changing hands every few weeks or days and were much too busy to be bothered with administrative details.

During these troubled months, the Saint was constantly on the move from city to city and from province to province, surrounded by an aureole of sanctity, untangling the miswoven threads of Fate and guiding Destiny on its appointed course.

One day in early winter in the Capital city on the second floor of a counting-house where the Neutral Party had its secret headquarters, the Leader sat in conference with his lieutenants.

"Gentlemen," he said, favoring them with a greasy smile, "we, the Neutral Party, are the rising star of the day. As you all know, there was a fairly even balance of power at the time the Old Order began to collapse.

Our forces were more numerous than those of the Conservatives and better equipped than those of the Radicals, but the consequences of a rash move would have been impossible to predict. This is no longer the case. The Conservatives and the Opposition, who were our only rivals worthy of serious mention, have succeeded in decimating each other. We who have hoarded our strength are now overwhelmingly superior to all our enemies combined. Our patience has paid its dividends. The time has come to strike."

The party lieutenants applauded. The Leader rubbed his hands and smiled. "Gentlemen," he continued, "I've called this caucus today to announce the successful termination of Stage Two of the Master Plan and officially to inaugurate Stage Three." He paused, and there was another round of sycophantic applause.

"However, there are some minor changes we must discuss before Stage Three goes into operation. As introduction, may I call upon the Commander of Kalopolis, who has a very interesting report to present?"

"Yes, Leader.," said the Commander of the Kalopolis Chapter of the conspiracy, in private life a successful usurer. He shuffled some papers, adjusted his spectacles, and began: "Gentlemen, fellow Neutrals, as I've mentioned in my earlier communiques, the Kalopolis Chapter of our Organization has been experimenting for some time with a secret weapon which one of our quick-thinking field workers managed to capture from the Scarecrow, a Radical inventor who has inadvertently supplied us with several other secret weapons. Our great Leader has wisely rejected the Scarecrow's previous—ah—contributions, as too destructive of life and property, but now, at last, we have a weapon which our experiments have proven fully operational, and which has received our Leader's unqualified approval."

"Will you describe how you seized control in Kalopolis, please," the Leader requested.

The Commander of Kalopolis smiled ingratiatingly and continued. "I'm almost at a loss," he said. "Paradoxically, the Figure—as its inventor chose to call it—is a weapon of peace and not a weapon of war at all. Its operation has thus far defied analysis, and our Leader has not granted permission for our researchers to dismantle it for more thorough study, but I can give you such data as is available. At the suggestion of an unidentified informant, we mounted the Figure on a standard, with portraits of our Leader on either side and sent a contingent of fifty minutemen to carry it to the gates of the Kalopolis Arsenal. Our entire force was ready in reserve in case the results were negative, but the precaution proved unnecessary. Just as our unidentified informant predicted, when the Conservative soldiers saw the Figure and the portraits, they opened the gates to us and threw down their arms.

We have controlled that province ever since. Radicals have attacked us six times. Moderates four times, Conservatives once, and a faction called the Southern Gentlemen, twice. On all such occasions, we merely display the Figure at the gate of the Arsenal. Invariably, the attackers desert in a body and apply for membership in our Organization, although, of course, only a small portion of them meet the requirements which our Leader has prescribed. That, gentlemen, is the main substance of my report. I'm prepared to answer any questions."

"Thank you," said the Leader. "That will be sufficient for the time being. I think the Commander's report clarifies the points I wish to raise in regard to the Master Plan at the present—"

There was a tap at the door, and a partisan soldier entered.

"Excuse the interruption, Leader," he said, "but there's someone here to see you on extremely urgent business."

"Have him wait," ordered the Leader. "Now, gentlemen—"

"It really is very important, Leader," said the minuteman.

"Who is he, and what does he want?"

"It's hard to explain, Leader. I really think you'd better see him."

"If it's important enough to warrant interrupting this meeting —" the Leader began, but just then, the Saint entered, on his own authority.

"Salvete," he greeted pleasantly.

"Why," gasped the Commander of Kalopolis, "this man is our unidentified informant!"

The Leader did not hear him. "A holy man! A stooge of our Conservative enemies! Who let you in?"

The Saint overlooked the question, as well as the patently ridiculous accusation.

"I have come," he said sweetly, "to advise you on a matter of Destiny, which concerns you and your Party."

"We're not interested," said the Leader. "Guard, escort him out, and see to it that no one else is admitted while I'm in conference."

"I couldn't help admitting him, Leader," said the soldier, "and I don't think I can throw him out, either. We already tried—or attempted to try."

The Leader rose, glowering, balled his fists, and opened his mouth to shout something, but the Saint raised his hand restrainingly, and the Leader discovered he could not make a sound. His mouth worked noiselessly, and a look of astonishment and frustration crossed his oily features.

"Peace," said the Saint, "I shall only take a few minutes of your time."

The Leader sat down. The Saint lowered his hand.

"Whatever you have to say," the Leader snarled, "say it and be off so that we can get on with the urgent business you've interrupted."

"As you wish," said the Saint. "The Universe has sent me to advise you that the Neutral Party, as presently constituted, is an anomaly in Destiny's Plan. It was never destined to exist, and therefore it cannot be."

There was a startled hush. The Neutral dignitaries looked angrily at the Saint, then hopefully at the Leader.

"What gibberish is this?" the Leader demanded. "If we can't be, then how do you account for the fact that we're the most powerful faction left in the Empire?" He tried to sound stern, but there was a quaver of doubt in his voice.

"That is not a fact," said the Saint, "but a sensory illusion. You are neutral, and that which is neutral has no existence except in the minds of men, for the elemental substance of reality is an equipoise of positive and negative antitheses. I am sorry."

"We call ourselves Neutrals," said the Leader, worried, "but only to distinguish ourselves from the Feudalists and the Radicals. We're a positive force for progress; 'Neutral' is just a name, a label, a designation."

"The Conservatives and the Opposition have antithetical principles," explained the Saint, "and between these two extremes, there can be neither compromise nor alternative. That which is neutral in precept, as your party is by the Will of the Universe, cannot be balanced against an antithesis, therefore cannot act. It is like a spade without soil or an hourglass without time. It has no place in the fabric of existence." He sighed. "It is so difficult to explain these things in terms comprehensible to the mortal mind. Even I, who am enlightened, only barely understand them."

Further quibbling was obviously pointless. The Leader and his lieutenants looked crushed. "How can we explain this?" moaned the Leader. "How can we face our fellow conspirators, even long enough to dissolve the Organization?"

"That will not be necessary," said the Saint compassionately. "The Universe has foreseen your difficulty and has arranged for its solution. Your anomalous organization has already split up into several smaller factions, all with different names. There is no Neutral Party."

He paused by the door on his way out and lifted his hand in blessing. "There never was a Neutral Party," he added softly as he left the room.

TWENTY-ONE

THE SCARECROW, AZAZA, AND THE TURTLE

The Scarecrow spent several months wandering around the countryside, living on whatever he could find, and only occasionally coming to his senses enough to remember his grief and his fury. When he finally began to associate with humanity again, the contact was only peripheral. He sat by the highway, begging alms of the southbound refugees.

Winter set in, and the Scarecrow's threadbare robe did not keep much of the wind out. His vigil by the highway was frozen misery, colder even than his woodland haunts. Whenever he amassed a few coppers for a bowl of soup, he slunk away to an inn on the outskirts of the village. He was not welcome there, but as long as he bought something, he was grudgingly allowed to stay inside out of the wind long enough to eat and sometimes long enough to warm himself.

The rare hours of sanity were the hardest, for then he was forced to realize he could not possibly live through the winter—he was half dead already, and the coldest months were ahead of him— and that for the rest of his brief life, he had nothing to look forward to but snow and wind and hunger. He had nothing left to live for, and therefore no particular objection to dying, but the process of death was uncomfortable, and in his efforts to avoid freezing and starving, he inadvertently stayed alive. He ate thin soup when the passing refugees were generous and roots and acorns when they were not. Sometimes he slept in woodsheds or chicken coops, and when he was chased out of these accommodations, he spent the night in hollow logs or under heaps of the driest leaves he could find in the woods. Whatever he ate, if anything, and wherever he slept, he was always bitterly disappointed when he awoke each morning, blue and brittle with cold, to find himself still alive.

One afternoon a blowing snow drove all but the hardiest travelers off the road, but fortune favored the Scarecrow's begging in spite of the light traffic. Toward the close of day, he put in an appearance at the inn, frozen and miserable, and stopped by the kitchen for his usual bowl of gruel. His luck was unbelievably good that day: the innkeeper's simple-hearted daughter added a small piece of bread to his order when her father was not looking.

Whimpering with gratitude, the Scarecrow faded away to an obscure corner to eat. He sat on the floor next to the wall, not presuming to occupy a chair. When he had finished his thin repast and licked the bowl clean to glean every calorie, he sat very quietly and hoped he would not be noticed for a while. The innkeeper could not stand the sight of him, and usually ordered him out the minute he finished eating, but today, apparently, the inclement weather and the Scarecrow's obvious misery had softened the man's ogrish heart a little, for he pretended not to notice the Scarecrow crouched in a dim corner.

More patrons drifted in, and a crowd collected. As the Scarecrow thawed superficially and regained full awareness of his surroundings, he began to watch the other people in the inn and listen to their unguarded conversation. Most of the talk was of current events—the many wars which ravaged the land, the mutual slaughter of the armies which should have been united against the barbarians, and the probable end of all civilized society. Although the topics were gloomy, the talk itself was cheerfully detached, as though the rapid decay of the world could not really involve anyone in that cozy inn.

Not everyone there even interested in these serious matters. At a nearby table, two irresponsible young blades from the village were drinking light wine and extolling the charms of the town siren, a young woman who—the Scarecrow gathered from the conversation—had arrived in the area a few months before from the big city, driven from her native habitat by some reverse of fortune.

The two swains speculated on the mystery of her past and differed in their theories but found themselves in wholehearted agreement on her ravishing beauty and the incomparable finesse of her professional technique.

At another table near the Scarecrow's corner, a holy man sat reading a book, frowning with intense concentration, oblivious to the medley of voices. He followed the print with one forefinger. His face seemed familiar, somehow, but the Scarecrow could not place it. The monkish habit reminded him of the Saint and all his empty talk of Destiny. Destiny! The Scarecrow sighed bitterly as he thought of the wretched state to which his preposterous destiny had reduced him.

He sighed again when he noticed the title of the holy man's book: *A Critique of Classical Casuistic Precepts from the Socioeconomic Viewpoint*. The Scarecrow had written it himself, and he wanted to warn the holy man about the subtle fallacy embodied in the central thesis, which he himself had not discovered until the book was already published and distributed. But he kept quiet, knowing he would not be believed. Who would ever believe that he, a ragged beggar, had once been among the most eminent savants in the Empire, with several erudite monographs in print? It was unfortunate that a man who seemed to have a sincere desire to improve his education should fall victim to the speciously well-documented treatise, but there was nothing to be done.

The Scarecrow's attention was diverted again by one of the young blades at the table, who said, quietly but urgently, "I think I just caught sight of her through the front window. She sometimes hangs out here when business is slow. If she comes in, shall we try to pick her up? Do you have any money?"

Eager for a look at this popular young woman, the Scarecrow craned his neck to watch the door.

"I was right, "said the youth. "It's her."

Small wonder these yokels were impressed; it was Azaza! The Scarecrow's heart pounded wildly; he nearly fainted. It was every inch Azaza, his unrequited obsession of the stormy and all-too-recent past, as unobtainably beautiful as ever. He wanted to jump up and shout her name, but he restrained himself with a violent effort. He still had a buried spark of pride; he had been ragged and starving in the old days, but never like this. Probably Azaza would not even recognize him, but if she did... He shuddered, covered his face with the empty wooden bowl, and wept in brokenhearted frustration.

He heard a chair scrape. One of the youths stood up and called to Azaza. The Scarecrow heard her voice answer, and then her light footsteps approaching. He cringed, trying to flatten himself into the baseboard, hoping Azaza would not see him.

She did not even glance in his direction. She joined the wastrels at their table, accepted their offer of a glass of wine, and entered into an exchange of light, affectionate banter. The Scarecrow sat still, listening and suffering. He wanted to scream and tear his hair, or ram his head through the wall, or strangle himself, or (more reasonably) to escape to the woods where he could vent his searing emotions without bothering people, but he dared not move.

He peeked cautiously around the soup-bowl. Azaza sat not more than three cubits away from him, rather unseasonably clothes in a diaphanous dress which concealed little or nothing depending on the light. Her voluptuous figure was silhouetted maddeningly against the warm glow of the hearth. The Scarecrow's head swam, and the throb of his heart was deafening.

He could bear no more. He had to get out of there before he lost his mind. He also had to leave inconspicuously, for if Azaza recognized him in his present circumstances, he felt he would die of shame. Her condescending pity had always been harder to bear than her most discourteous rebuffs, even when he had had a few delusions of personal worth.

Slowly, carefully, silently, the Scarecrow rose to a crouch and edged along the wall, away from Azaza's table. Inch by inch, he retreated, keeping his face covered with his soup bowl, with only one eye exposed, longingly to savor Azaza's beauty. When he was far enough away to feel safer, he stood up. Azaza's back was to him now, and he thought he could reach the front door without her seeing him. He stepped forward hesitantly, looking back over his shoulder. Still unable to tear his gaze from Azaza, he took another step.

He stumbled over an outstretched foot and fell with a crash. Every eye in the place must be on him now, he thought unhappily, as he lay face down on the floor. He estimated that he had almost fallen into the studious holy man's lap. That would really have been embarrassing!

"Really, my good man," boomed a resonant masculine voice, "you'll hurt yourself if you're not more careful. Are you all right?"

The Scarecrow stiffened, and Azaza was suddenly forgotten. He knew that voice! He leaped to his feet, shaking with revitalized hatred of years before. The 'holy man' had looked up from his reading, marking the place with one forefinger, and was solicitously watching him stand up.

"It's the Turtle!" the Scarecrow cried, "betrayer of the working class, lackey of the right-thinking tyrants! I thought that face was familiar!"

"Hey, lunatic!" shouted the innkeeper, striding angrily to the scene of the disturbance, "nobody gave you leave to insult my customers! I should have known better than to let you clutter up my establishment for so long!"

"It's the Turtle himself!" shrilled the Scarecrow. "That bogus priest is the Turtle! I'd know that face anywhere! He owes me forty crowns for the armor I sold him years ago!"

"Please don't pay any attention to him, father," said the innkeeper, picking the Scarecrow up by the collar. "He was addled when he first came to our village, and he's grown steadily worse ever since. He doesn't mean any harm."

The Turtle, still marking his place with his forefinger, took it all in with raised eyebrows, puzzled by the Scarecrow's outburst. The Scarecrow dangled by the collar from the innkeeper's beefy hand, still clutching the empty wooden bowl, and pointed a long, skeletal arm and forefinger at the impostor.

"Believe me!" he screamed frantically, raising his voice half an octave. "I know what I'm saying! I know his face! I know his voice! It's our enemy, the enemy of the common people throughout the Empire, commander of the police who tramples our rights, ally of the tax-collectors who wrest the bread from our mouths! I swear he's wearing armor under that disguise—the same armor I stupidly sold him, and for which he still owes me forty crowns balance! All who hear my voice. I call you to witness!"

With these words, he raised the soup-bowl, and, to everyone's horror, let fly at the Turtle. The bowl bounced from the Turtle's chest with a muffled clang. There was a gasp from the onlookers.

The Turtle sprang to his feet, dropping *A Critique of Classical Casuistic Precepts from the Socioeconomic Viewpoint*, and losing his place.

"Great Zas," he roared, "I really am the Turtle! I remember everything! The Empire is flying to pieces, and here I sit, thinking I'm a holy man! I must get back to the Capital at once!" He peeled off the hooded robe, beneath which he was still in the full panoply of war.

"Beloved!" cried Azaza, dashing across the room to throw her arms around the Turtle's neck. "At last, I've found you! I thought I'd lost you forever!"

The dumbfounded innkeeper released the Scarecrow, who fell to the floor with a bony clatter. He was back on his feet in an instant. He leaped to the tabletop, where he crouched as though about to spring, and pointed the accusing arm and finger.

"Pay me those forty crowns, you prince of deadbeats!

Enjoy your brutal oppression, multiply your disgusting crimes against working-class decency, grind our lacerated faces with ingenious new atrocities of legal abuse and rob us of the few rights we still have, but at least pay your debts!"

Azaza emerged from the Turtle's embrace and turned.

"Why it's the Scarecrow!" she exclaimed. "Scarecrow, how you've changed!"

The Scarecrow had another salvo of invectives all necked and aimed, but they died in his throat as his eyes met Azaza's. This was exactly, precisely, identically what he had wanted so desperately to avoid, and in his enthusiasm for unmasking the Turtle, he had forgotten all about it. His outstretched arm sagged, his gaunt face glowed, and his aggressive crouch melted into a fearful cringe. He climbed off the table and slunk away to the far end of the room.

But now, the other people in the inn were recovering from their initial confusion and realizing that for once, the Scarecrow must have said something valid. As Azaza and the Turtle went into another passionate clinch, a muttering arose and grew in volume.

"It really is the Turtle!"

"His bona fide Potency!"

"The Supreme Commander!"

"Avowed enemy of wrong-thinkers!"

"Enemy of the common people—all common people!"

"Our enemy!"

"Running dog of the feudalists!"

"Oppressor of the poor!"

"That's us!"

"Let's kill him!"

In answer to this suggestion, there was a lusty roar of approval. Azaza and the Turtle separated in alarm and turned to see the angry rabble closing in. Knives flashed. Cudgels menaced. Teeth were bared.

The Turtle slipped a protective arm around Azaza and looked around for a route of strategic withdrawal, but the doors and windows were all blocked by the threatening mob. The Turtle drew his sword. Confronted with real fighting steel, the mob paused for a second—but only for a second. The Turtle was a symbol of everything the corrupt aristocracy had taught them to hate, and their own voices had roused them to insensate fury.

"Kill!" someone shouted.

"KILL!" came the answering roar.

"Hold it," cried the Turtle, raising his hand. "There's a word I would say! We can talk this over sensibly!"

"KILL!" thundered the mob. "BLOOD! DEATH! VENGEANCE!"

"Hold!" bellowed the Turtle in a voice of great authority.

"Don't force me to harm someone in self-defense when it's not necessary! Attack later if you still think you must, but first, hear me out! Let's .be broadminded about this!"

There was a collective yell of raw, bestial hatred, and the rabble closed in, swinging cudgels and broken bottles. Azaza screamed. The Turtle had no room to ply his sword and was immediately buried under a mass of rabid assailants.

From across the room, the Scarecrow watched with mixed feelings. He was quite embarrassed by all the trouble he had started, and being at heart an idealist, he would have much preferred to see his old enemy guillotined after a fair trial by a revolutionary court, but the horrible scene of mob fury had its brighter side as well. A blow struck by commoners against nobility was, *ipso facto*, a blow for freedom and a good thing.

From the midst of the scuffle, sounding above the grunts, yells, and whacks, there issued a resounding crack of skull against skull, and the Turtle hurled two limp bodies back into the crowd. A moment later, there was another bony crack, and two more casualties flew back into the arms of their comrades. Then two more. The Turtle had lost his temper.

Another bloodthirsty war cry shook the building, but this time the front rank of rabble resisted the encouraging shoves from behind, and the Turtle gained a breathing space. He leaped to the top of the nearest table, where he sheathed his sword in a swift, dramatic gesture and held up his hands for silence.

The simple villagers recognized real courage when they saw it, and it was a quality they could admire even in their enemies. The roar died down to a chorus of snarls and growls, then to a mutter.

"Hear me out!" cried the Turtle in a stentorian voice. "When you've heard my side, then attack again if you still deem it necessary, but first let me speak on my own behalf! Let us not allow our minds to be ruled by mob passions!"

After another brief several-throated growl, there was comparative quiet, broken only by the groans of the reviving casualties. When the Turtle saw he had the floor, he struck an oratorical pose and began to speak.

"My friends," he pronounced, "we represent opposing views on a deep and burning issue. It is an extremely important issue. It is perhaps the most significant conflict of views that we—the Empire —the civilized world—nay, all humanity in all history—have faced and been forced to resolve. It is a question over which friendships have been sundered, houses have been divided, oaths have been sworn, blood has been spilled, brave men have lost their lives, and this great Empire, our beloved homeland, has been split into countless warring factions. It is a burning issue indeed.

"Let us pause for a few moments to take thought, to analyze this great burning issue over which formerly civilized men have found it necessary to become merciless slayers. Let us examine this question in its several phases, even without immediate hope of resolving it, to be sure that at least we really understand it. Let us, for these few thoughtful moments, behave like our more usual decent, civilized selves. Perhaps, after all has been said, it will still appear to us that our views, the opposing sides of this great ideological conflict, can, in fact, be settled only by unthinking violence. But perhaps this is not inevitable, as it quite naturally seems to many of us now, in the heat of our auger. Perhaps, somewhere among the shibboleths which cloud this great, burning issue of the day, there may yet be found a fundamental meeting ground of our minds, some basic, instinctive ideal, common to all civilized men, upon which—antithetical though our views may seem—we can agree and sympathize.

"I think so. I also think it not impossible that this fundamental precept, universal to all our natures and beliefs, may prove to be of sufficiently broad scope that we shall actually be able to put aside our differences, at least for the moment, and join forces long enough to save this great civilization of ours from the frightful cataclysm which is currently tearing it limb from limb.

"History cries out to us, my friends! In the midst of its death-throes, it implores our aid! Is this a call to fight? Yes, most emphatically, but is it not also a call to think before we fight? We must come to grips with this great—and still imperfectly defined—power of evil and destruction and vanquish it, but first, we must make plans. 'Aha,' our critics sneer, 'what has ever been accomplished just by thinking about it? We want action,' they will say; 'there's been enough of this idle philosophizing.'

"But has there been? My friends, surely we are all intelligent enough to see through such specious criticism. I condemn all such self-styled men of action—impulsive ruffians who dare to scoff at our policy of thoughtful foresight. What has been the result of hasty action? Observe the state of the Empire! These 'men of action'—and I include Conservatives as well as wrong-thinkers—have battled over ideologies while the real enemies cut them down from the rear and now are battling again over whose fault it was!

"Yes, fellow citizens, the time has come for constructive action; the time has come for battle and for victory, but in taking up arms, we must not betray the glorious heritage we have fearlessly undertaken to defend—a heritage not only of courage but also of wisdom. The founders of our Empire were men of iron indeed—nay, men of Damascus steel—but they were also men of gold, men who possessed not only the strength and the valor to take up arms in a just and honorable war, but also the self-respect to demand a worthy cause to fight for, and the discernment to tell a genuine Cause from an empty slogan! In short, they were not only fighting men but thinking men!

"For this, fellow citizens, do I condemn our critics, the so-called men of action. By failing to take thought when thought was most urgently needed, they have betrayed not only the past—our famous heritage—but they have also betrayed the present—the Empire! For what they have done to our homeland. I accuse!"

The Turtle thundered on while his listeners stared in hypnotized attention, unconsciously mimicking his successive facial expressions. Knives were slipped back into their sheaths, and cudgels were set aside—very quietly, so not to cause the slightest disturbance. Although not everyone was sure just what he was talking about, it was perfectly obvious that he, and he alone of all the demagogues in the Empire, was talking plain sense.

The Turtle closed in on his subject gradually, for it was highly controversial, to say the least. He began with matters that seemed peripheral, even irrelevant, to the few who stopped to wonder. He spoke of earthy fundamentals: the warmth of summer, the clean snows of winter, the fresh air, the blue sky. He spoke of spring planting, the germination of seeds, the ripening of crops, autumn harvests, and the bounty of the earth. He reaffirmed the essential dignity of honest labor and confided that although he was a noble, he too had been reared on the land. He treated of honest rest after honest work and a well-earned evening repast of wholesome country fare. All these things, he explained, were the building-stones of which the lofty edifice of civilized Empire had been constructed.

Then he branched off into other relevant subjects: the former might of the Empire, the greatness of its traditions, the intrinsic superiority of its language and customs, the solid, old-fashioned virtues of its citizens, and their prestige among the underprivileged inhabitants of barbarian countries beyond the frontiers. He extolled the prowess of the Empire's warriors, who—he added sternly—were not craven hirelings like the soldiers of other lands, but plain, honest citizens like himself, who had entered the service of the Empire out of a loyal desire to serve the great institution of which they knew they were a part.

His voice conveyed conspiratorial intimacy with his audience. Carefully, systematically, couching controversial subjects in euphemistic terms, he explained the principles of Dynamic Feudalism from the ground up. He outlined the history of the

Empire and recounted the deeds of the ancient kings and knights who had welded forty-one warring states into one vast, invincible Empire. He told of their courage and their wisdom—especially their wisdom—and explained how an unbroken chain of noble chromosomes linked them with the modern aristocracy. He touched delicately on noblesse oblige and the Divine Right of Kings.

This was too much for the Scarecrow. "Reactionary propaganda!" he jeered, unable to restrain himself. "What a pitiful fabric of pseudoscience our oppressors have devised to mask their degeneration! He's trying to befog our minds with high-sounding prattle! He's using psychology on us! Throw him· out, but first, make him give me my forty crowns!"

The Turtle looked hurt and a little bewildered, as he always was when unexpectedly contradicted. His train of thought was broken. It was a tense moment.

Azaza rose to the emergency. "Let's get rid of that noisy heckler!" she cried.

This impressed everyone as a sensible suggestion.

There was a brief scuffle between the Scarecrow and a pair of stocky blacksmiths. The Scarecrow flew out the door, skidded on the packed snow covering the pavement, and fell. He picked himself up and went to watch and listen at the front window. The worst feature of his new vantage point was that now he had a clear view of Azaza, and every rapturous look she gave the Turtle was another painful barb in the Scarecrow's heart.

The Turtle resumed as if nothing had happened and spoke for another twenty minutes. He summarized what he had already expatiated and underlined the undeniable conclusion that if there was to be a civilization and a government, there had to be men of gold to direct it. The audience nodded enthusiastically and made noises of agreement.

The Turtle sighed volcanically, put one fist to his brow, and regretted that the nobility of the Empire had been exterminated almost to a man in the recent pandemic of irresponsible uprisings by men who would never have done such a foolish thing had they only taken time to think. A murmur of regret went up from the audience. The Turtle wiped away a tear and found he was too overcome with emotion to proceed. While he recovered, the people whispered among themselves. It really was disgraceful, they told one another, that the nobles had been dealt such a scurvy blow by the very people to whose welfare they had altruistically dedicated their lives, though for some reason none of the villagers had ever viewed the problem in quite that light before.

When the Turtle cleared his throat and resumed, his voice was no longer hushed and sad. His brow clouded fiercely, and in his tone was the warlike rumble of drums.

"The nobles of the Empire are gone!" he cried, "yet we must carry on. Who will take their places? Who will lead us? There must be someone in this broad land of ours, with the fortitude to assume the burden of rule!"

He looked around. There were whispers but no volunteers.

"Where, then, did our original nobility arise?" the Turtle roared rhetorically. "They did not drop from the sky. What was their origin and their ancestry? Most importantly, are there more such men somewhere, to whom we can appeal in this hour of peril?"

The Turtle studied the faces of his audience. Their wide eyes and bated breath left no doubt that he had succeeded in awakening their minds—in making them think. Now it remained only to tell them what to think.

His voice dropped to a vibrant stage-whisper.

"They rose from the common people and earned their own titles—Don't scoff! It's a matter of history, and in this underrated fact lies the very principle upon which our Empire was founded. Let me emphasize, once again, that Dynamic Feudalism is nothing new. It's not just another ideology, made up to order by some special interest group to lend respectability to its own selfish ends. If the truth be told, it is far more conservative than the political doctrines of many who would call us liberals, for Dynamic Feudalism dates back to the foundation of civilization and is the system from which modern feudalism evolved. Our late Emperor, of illustrious memory, has set the precedent in modern times which will make the aristocracy not only self-perpetuating, but self-replacing in times of emergency such as the present, and it was an act of far-sighted statesmanship not soon to be forgotten by a grateful posterity. Now, let me repeat my question: The aristocracy is decimated, and the Empire is without leadership. Who will pick up the fallen banners and fill the breach?"

There was more excited whispering.

"Now," said the Turtle sternly, "now that the Empire lies in defenseless ruin to await the arrival of its barbarian destroyers, why, I ask, can there not arise a new nobility, a new Conservative Army, who will follow the heroic example set by the founders of our Empire; who will drive out the barbarians, discipline the wrong-thinking factions, rebuild our social order on its original principles, and then take its rightful and well-earned place as the new aristocracy?"

The audience cheered. When the clamor had died, the innkeeper spoke up: "That's well and sensibly spoken, sir, and I'm sure everyone here agrees we should all pitch in and give the Dynamic Feudalist Party our full support. But tell us one thing: Where will this great new army arise? To judge from what news comes our way, there isn't an army of any faction left, strong enough to attempt the great feats you've outlined."

"A good question," the Turtle replied, "An excellent question indeed. As a matter of fact, I was on the point of venturing a tentative answer to that very question, an answer—a mere suggestion. I should call it—which I hoped might also shed some light on the central issue of modern times—the great ideological conflict which has challenged the wisdom and energies of the whole civilized world. And yet...perhaps I'm wrong. Perhaps the plan is too visionary, even in view of the recent precedent set by our late Emperor. I'm almost afraid to answer, now that the question has been so clearly put, for fear of your disapproval."

"Speak!" cried the innkeeper.

"SPEAK!" echoed everyone.

The Turtle strode back and forth within the limited confines of the tabletop, frowning thoughtfully as he searched for the perfect phrases. Finally, he faced his audience again, and they awaited the oracle in breathless silence.

"Citizens of the Empire!" said the Turtle, "as the good innkeeper has pointed out, no existing army is prepared to answer the clarion. Obviously, a new army must be recruited, and the question is, where? But is it not equally obvious that the restorers of moral government, the soldiers of the Citizens' Conservative Army, must grow from the Empire's fertile soil—must arise from the common citizenry, as in antiquity? They must be fearless men, yet circumspect; idealistic yet practical, and although possessed of the initiative to make places for themselves in the world, yet they must have the moral stamina to resist the temptations of high office."

He spread his arms. "Who best fills these rigid qualifications?" he thundered, in the voice he had developed while drilling troops in regimental formation. "Who is worthy of the trust? Who has the physical courage and the moral character to become the officers, the hardcore, of the Citizens' Conservative Army? Who, indeed, but the stalwart yeomanry of this fair village!"

A wild cheer arose, blasting from every lung and rocking the sturdy timbers of the inn. The outcry brought people from all over the hamlet to see what was the occasion for such rejoicing in an otherwise dismal world. Cheering and whistling, the villagers lifted the Turtle to their shoulders, table and all, so parade through the streets, hailing him as their commander and the Empire's liberator.

While runners dispersed to spread the news throughout the countryside and round up recruits, the innkeeper painted a sign on an old bedsheet and hung it on the facade of the inn. It read:

THE EMPIRE NEEDS YOU, YOU. AND YOU!
ENLIST NOW!
CITIZENS' CONSERVATIVE ARMY!

When the gathering crowd overflowed the inn, he provided wood for an enormous bonfire out in the street. He tapped several kegs of his finest brew and passed out free steinsful to everyone who pledged to join the Turtle's campaign.

People brought drums and brasswinds to lead the singing and marching, and the rally went on all night. By morning, the roll bore the signatures of over two hundred stouthearted villagers and ploughboys. Some came armed with antique swords and shields they had found in their attics and quaint, old-fashioned bronze armor. Some carried hunting bows and rustic quarterstaffs. The majority reported in armed with rakes and hoes, wearing saucepans for helmets. Their patriotic spirit, however, was just short of fanatic, and the Turtle was well pleased with them.

Early in the morning, before his merry men had a chance to develop hangovers, the Turtle purchased a horse for himself and arranged transportation for Azaza.

TWENTY-TWO

THE PATRIARCH

"*Der groesste Feind des Menschenwohl,*" quoth the
    Patriarch of Kalopolis, raising his goblet,
    "*Das ist und bleibt der Alkohol.*
    "*Doch in der Bibel steht geschrieben:*
    "'*Du sollst auch deine Feinde lieben.*"
    He turned to Melli, who sped into the library with another load
of bottles. "How that kid's changed since his enlightenment," he
complained. "He was a nice kid, twenty years ago. He even had a
sense of humor in those days."

Melli set the new supply of wines and liquors on the floor by
the table. There was no other space for them; the rest of the library
already blazed with color from the rows and clusters of bottles, full
or partly full of sweet wine, dry wine, red wine, white wine, amber
wine, rose wine, tawny wine, sparkling wine, still wine, crackling
wine and petillant wine, interspersed with containers of beer, ale,
stout, cider, mead, whiskey, brandy, rum, gin, vodka, aquavit, sake,
tequila, arrack, pulque, chichi and okolehao, all massed in colorful
cheer on the table, on the chairs, on the bookshelves in front of the
books, and on the floor all around the walls. The aged Patriarch
cackled happily as he moved about the room, thoughtfully sampling
a little of each in accordance with this newest theory of epis-
temology.

"Yes, he was a nice kid. I loved him like my own son. I taught him all the theology he knows, except for what has to come straight from the Universe. He was the life of the party in those days—let's see, how long ago?...he was thirty-nine by the time I had him in shape to go to the mountains and seek enlightenment. This town lost something when he left. He played the guitar like nobody before or since. You never heard anything like it; any tune you could name, classics or pops. Those wire guitar-strings are his own invention. I think—so is the pick, incidentally; the heathen Spaniards, who claim credit for inventing guitars, use their finger-tips instead of the pick. You can trust a heathen to do things the hard way. They make strings out of rabbit-entrails, or something equally unsanitary—I don't remember for sure, Pretty primitive, eh?"

Melli shrugged.

"He was a handsome kid and full of fun. He could drink anybody under the table, except me and one or two others. Verily, those were the days. I don't know what could have gotten into him. Enlightenment never affected me like that, except maybe temporarily. Well, *faber est quisque suae fortunae*, to coin a hack-neyed phrase. I just hope he outgrows his attitude someday. In fact, I hope he outgrows it in a hurry because he's destined to head back to the monastery, week after next, and presumably, we'll be dead by then."

He drained a flask into his goblet and shook his ancient head sadly. "Chaos, chaos everywhere; his work's about done. I'm afraid. I'm glad the Neutrals—or whatever they call the local organization since my boy broke up their party—have been able to hold this town. They're wrong-thinking screwballs like everyone else these days, but I'll give them their due for the peace and quiet. Yes, my boy's work is done, and civilization is doomed. The Church will go down with it, of course, then he and I can both retire—unless I still contrive to stop him."

He moved down the line of bottles and came to the ones Melli had just brought in. "Oho!" he said, "some of these look interesting. You've found wines in that cellar that I'd forgotten existed. What would I do without you?"

He sighed and changed the subject again. "I don't know what

we'll do when the heathens get here. Melli. *Dulce et decorum est pro patria mori.* I guess. They're still coming, and no one's even tried to oppose them. They'll reach the Capital in a week or ten days, and after that, it won't take them more than another week to get here. How much that Figure contraption of the Neutrals' slows them down remains to be seen. It doesn't matter so much to you and me; I'm along in years and wouldn't have lived much longer anyway, and no heathen could ever catch you. Still, folks have enjoyed all these centuries of peace, and I hate to see the Empire go under."

He drained the goblet. Melli opened another flask and replenished it for him.

"You know, Melli. I've been expounding on heathens for decades now, and yet I've never seen one. I used to think I had. Sixty-five years ago, when I was an acolyte, the Seminary used to bring a heathen in once each term and show him off to the class. "'*Discipuli,*' the professor would tell us, '*bene spectate,*' and remember we'd all be like this wretch if it weren't for the Church! Then we students would look the heathen over and take notes, and he'd growl at us if we got too close. We'd try to ask him questions, and he'd answer '*Mi vin ne komprenas, frato,*' no matter what we asked. And do you know, it wasn't until years later, when I had an assistant professorship in the same school, that I found out it was all rigged? That heathen was just a hired actor. Good make-up job, though—the dirt under his fingernails looked almost real. Anyway, Melli, to this day, I've never actually seen a heathen. It's an educational gap the heathens will soon fill for me; I suppose when they come howling in the front gate."

He paused in his circuit to gaze out the window. "To think that a disciple of mine would grow up to be the arch-iconoclast of all time! Something certainly went wrong with that boy's enlightenment. I don't mean he's not a saint—far from it; he's a saint among saints and no question about it. What I mean is...well, no, that's not it...or maybe it is. Maybe it's the closest I can come to what I mean, in language the unenlightened would understand. I mean, I think Destiny's making a mistake! Something's gone haywire with the Plan! I've got to find that mistake and set it straight before it's too late to save the Church."

He resumed wandering about the library. He stopped by the table and picked up a bottle of raw-looking clear liquid. He held it up to the light and shook it.

"Maybe this stuff the barbarians drink has the answer," he said. He handed the bottle to Melli, who opened it and poured for him. The Patriarch sampled it and smacked his lips critically.

"An uncouth, empirical sort of wisdom," he pronounced. "Let's try something else."

He indicated the room full of bottles with a sweep of his hand. Melli had to help him regain his balance. "All the world's knowledge is here in these flasks," he said. "In taking this cross-section of my wine-cellar—the finest wine-cellar in Kalopolis—it's just as though the keenest minds of every foreign land were here in the library, and I was talking with each in turn. This collection's been imported from every corner of the world, and somewhere here is the answer. I must have been out of my mind to think I could find it by staying sober."

He hiccoughed. "And all the while, I was just wasting time. The wisdom of the world is in its wines, and, of course, in our three hundred forty-five volumes of Scripture. The salvation of the Church is somewhere in these bottles and these books, and there may still be time to find it. Where's something I haven't tried yet?"

Melli handed him a small, flat bottle of rich amber-colored spirits and traced a question-mark in the air with one finger. The Patriarch took the bottle and squinted at the label.

"I don't know," he replied. "I can't read a word of it; it's in Japanese...Wait a minute; I think I've seen these same figures somewhere before. Probably in the Scripture. Everything's in the Scripture."

He veered to the bookcase and looked over the shelves of sacred literature. After some thought, he selected volume XLIII of the Book of Truth.

"I saw it right here somewhere," he said, turning pages, "in a footnote, I believe. It was just the other day that I ran across it, but I didn't pay much attention...Yes, here it is."

He compared the label on the bottle with the scriptural reference.

"Ah, so," he said, affecting an accent. "It's plum sake, imported from Western Kyushu. They manufacture the stuff at Tenmangu

Shrine in Daizaifu. Priests? Making wine? I wonder why we never thought of that! It's a lot more respectable than collecting tithes, as some cults do. They're heathen Shintos, of course, but it says here they make excellent booze, so they must be learned and saintly men. Open it. Melli, and let's see what they have to teach me."

TWENTY-THREE

AZAZA AND THE TURTLE

The Turtle's grassroots army marched on toward the Capital, growing as it went. There were a few brushes with partisan forces on the way, but very few. Even the most fanatic insurgents were tired of the indecisive warfare, and the more disillusioned they were, the more readily they succumbed to the Turtle's oratory. Whenever the army came to a town, and whenever they met a caravan of refugees, the Turtle called a halt and made a speech. This slowed their progress but added to their numbers, for the Turtle's commonsense patriotism always won the hearts of most of his listeners. When he spoke to Radical or Neo-Neutral attackers of a Conservative fief, they always abandoned the siege and joined him. Then he would appeal to the defenders, whereupon the embattled knights usually decided that Dynamic Feudalism was not nearly so dangerous a doctrine in the light of the existing circumstances as they had formerly believed, and they added their private forces to the Citizens' Conservative Army. In this way, the Turtle gained arms and armor, as well as warm bodies, and by the time they approached the Capital, a noticeable minority of the troops had collected enough equipage actually to look like soldiers. The Turtle organized these into his show company and taught them dismounted drill.

Those who still looked like rubes wearing saucepans on their heads were not discouraged and took no nonsense from the professionals. Whatever they looked like, they knew they were really soldiers, fighting for one of history's really worthwhile causes. Moreover, in the skirmishes with wrong-thinking war parties, rakes and shovels had proved to be formidable weapons, in experienced hands.

Azaza saw a great deal of the Turtle during the march, but never alone. He was always busy assimilating the new recruits who flocked to the standard, making speeches to enlist still more, orating fresh enthusiasm into the hearts of his troops, and making arrangements for the ever-thornier logistic problems of the swelling army.

Azaza would have been more than willing to share a tent with him, so they could be together once in a while. She made the suggestion herself, in fact, but the Turtle would not hear of it until after they were lawfully married.

"Then let's get married now," Azaza begged. "There'll be a priest in the next town, and it only takes a few minutes if you're too busy for a formal ceremony."

"Be patient, my dear," the Turtle told her. "When we've driven the barbarians out of the Empire, and the Hall of Kings has crowned me Emperor, then we'll be married by the Prime Ecclesiarch himself, and we'll be Emperor and Empress together. By then, we'll have had a respectable period of engagement, and that's very important. We of the nobility must watch our reputations carefully, you know; it's part of noblesse oblige."

"You know best, my love," Azaza conceded. The Turtle went out to make a speech, and Azaza consoled herself by thinking of the wealth of the Empire, the Empress's half of which would soon be hers.

TWENTY-FOUR

THE SECRETARY ROYAL

In the Hall of Kings, the debate continued. The delegates, blear-eyed, haggard, and hoarse as ravens, but resolved to make the most of their chance to express themselves, went on shouting, fuming, calling one another unpleasant names, and occasionally throwing things.

One day the Secretary Royal rose to add his voice to the babble, and by an incredible stroke of fortune, happened to begin speaking at a moment when everyone else who had the floor was pausing for rhetorical effect.

"Gentlemen," he intoned, "fellow delegates:"

Partly out of respect for the king's advanced years, and partly because it had become painful even to whisper through their raw throats, the rest of the speakers left off shouting and sat down to compose fresh material.

"I have an item of business," the Secretary Royal began, a little awed by the sudden silence but quick to make use of it. "Fortunately, it is brief and non-partisan. It is one of my duties as Secretary Royal to the Imperial Hall of Kings—I mention this for the benefit of our junior members, who at this moment are in the overwhelming majority—it is my duty twice a year to present a summary report of the last six months' accomplishments. It is a very ancient custom, bequeathed to us from the days when the Hall of

Kings convened for a few days semiannually. As the sessions lengthened and finally overlapped, the reading of the minutes took the form of this progress report. Some say it's an anachronism in modern times, but I've been presenting it faithfully for thirty years, and it means a great deal to me. Since I haven't been able to get a word in for some time, this one is three months overdue, and I'd greatly appreciate your attention for a few minutes while I get this matter off my mind."

He glanced around and was surprised again when there seemed to be no objections. The forty-one delegates were quaffing honey and lemon juice for their throats.

"After his late Radiance passed away," said the Secretary Royal, "it was disclosed at the reading of the imperial will that the Turtle, a newly-dubbed knight who was serving as Supreme Commander of the Imperial Regular Army, was to be installed as the rightful heir and successor to the imperial throne. Sir Turtle's mysterious disappearance at that time occasioned the appointment of an imperial investigating committee to look into the matter and make recommendations. The committee has not yet submitted a report, none of the committeemen are presently serving in the Hall of Kings, and there is no reason to believe there will ever be a report."

The delegates were wrapping hot towels around their anguished throats in hopes that it would help ease the pain.

"I proceed to item two," said the Secretary Royal. "It was moved and seconded that a provisional Emperor be chosen from our own midst to reign until the heir returned to claim his legacy, or for the space of three months, after which, if the heir had not returned, the provisional Emperor would be coronated as founder of the next dynasty. After some debate, the question was shelved since no candidate was able to poll a plurality.

"Item three: Shortly after the outbreak of the present disorder, it was again suggested that an Emperor be selected. The proposal was made by several junior members of this august body, all talking at once and at cross-purpose. The motion was carried by acclamation—which was irregular but perhaps technically legal—and there were forty-one nominations. A formal roll-call vote was impossible for want of an up-to-date roll, so I attempted to call the roll by provinces, an alternate procedure provided for in the Rules of Order. I was unable to tabulate the results of the election, however, because most of the candidates were simultaneously endeavoring to elect themselves by acclamation. There were several petitions demanding a recount before I had even given up trying to call the roll."

The Secretary Royal wiped his brow. The delegates were consulting with their aides and advisors, jotting notes for future addresses, and treating their throats. The Secretary Royal went on stoutly.

"Item four: It was moved and seconded—again by several delegates at once—that certain drastic reforms be made in the Rules of Order. No orderly debate on the matter was possible, since the authors of these revisions have insisted on putting the revisions into practice before they were made official, but the proposals are still under discussion."

The Secretary Royal paused again to look around at the delegates, who were still studiously outlining their next speeches, ignoring him completely.

"Item five:" said the Secretary Royal. "It was moved and seconded...on the other hand, what's the use?" He turned to his few remaining colleagues from the original representative body. "Shall we leave them here?" he suggested.

"May as well," replied another monarch. "We could have been on our way south by now."

"Just a minute while I adjourn us, then. According to the Rules of Order, we have to stay here as long as the Hall's in session."

The Secretary Royal turned back to the round table. He picked up an ordinary rawhide mallet which he had been using as a gavel and gave a whack that echoed for several seconds. The delegates all jumped and looked up with angry glares for the source of the disturbance.

"Gentlemen," the Secretary Royal announced, "I thank you for your kind attention. There remains but one matter of importance— an announcement which I believe may be of at least passing interest to all of us. The barbarians have crossed into this province and are headed straight for the Capital. They will be here in two days. The Empire has fallen, the Capital is doomed, civilization is destroyed, history has ended, and there is no conceivable remedy. Those of you who feel you can put your points across in the next two days are welcome to use this building for your debate. For the benefit of anyone who has sense enough to head south. I declare this session of the Imperial Hall of Kings indefinitely adjourned *sina die*."

He made a brief entry in the Archives and closed the volume. He removed his crown and set it carefully on the Round Table.

Just then, the great, satin-covered double door of the assembly chamber swung open, and a Conservative soldier rushed in.

"Your Majesties!" he shouted, "the Capital is saved!

We just got word that his Potency the Turtle is marching this way at the head of an enormous army; he'll arrive just ahead of the barbarians."

"Conservatives!" cried a Radical." We must flee for our lives!"

"Not exactly, your Majesty," said the soldier. "They're Dynamic Feudalists. The messenger who brought the word made it plain that all they plan to do is stop the barbarians and establish order. For what it's worth, the army's composed of ex-Radicals, ex-Neutrals, ex-everything; there are even a few nobles in it. I'm sorry to disturb your Majesties this way, but my captain thought you might like to know."

He saluted perfunctorily and left.

"Insolent varlet," said a Conservative king. "Why didn't he relay the message through the page whose office it is to interrupt our proceedings?"

"He probably couldn't find him," someone explained. "That page quit his job several months ago and went out to join some faction or other."

"What does the Turtle hope to gain by this?" asked the Secretary Royal. "Doesn't he realize he's too late? We gave him three months to come to claim his legacy."

"He's too late according to the resolutions of the Hall," amended one of his colleagues, "but the Emperor's will didn't set any such deadline, so there's something to be said on both sides."

"It would appear," said the Secretary Royal moodily, "that the repercussions of his Radiance's senility will haunt us for some time to come. During his dotage, he effected a complete revision of the Rules of Order, entirely at random, and managed to be out of order much of the time in spite of it. The Turtle is his creation, too; I'm sure I could have blocked his ennoblement if he hadn't had the Emperor on his side."

"Now it looks like he's going to be the new Emperor," said the Conservative. "Ironic turn of fate. When the Turtle disappeared, there wasn't a king in this Hall who didn't have a better claim to the throne."

"There still isn't," snarled the Secretary Royal. "Even among these crackpots, there still isn't a delegate that wouldn't be a better choice."

"Come now; you're letting your personal dislike for the Turtle get the best of you. He isn't that bad."

"There isn't another king or pseudo-king in this Hall," growled the Secretary Royal dogmatically, "that wants to promote soldiers to nobles. It's bad enough that our civilization has degenerated to the point that a commoner like the Turtle can join the army as a private and work his way up to blooded nobility—and it looks like he might go even further—but the very foundation of Dynamic Feudalism, as explained by the Turtle himself, is that any idiot who can swing a sword effectively should have a title and a coat of arms. How do you think he raised the army he has now, except by promising the soldiers titles?"

"Hmm," said the Conservative.

"We can't just let him take over the Empire like this. It would be the end of everything! Violent overthrow of our government will mean the end of the Empire. Even if the Turtle sets it up again exactly as it is now, it'll still be a different Empire, and the end of our history."

"Didn't you officially declare history at an end, a few minutes ago?"

"That was before we found out the barbarians were going to meet some opposition. There was no hope of stopping the barbarians, but there's a good chance of stopping the Turtle after he's stopped the barbarians, and the Empire will be preserved."

The Conservative studied the Secretary Royal's face, wondering if the strain had not finally snapped his reason; there was hardly anything rational in the man's eyes. But no, nothing could ever disrupt the hinge-like operation of that legalistic mind.

"If the Turtle's army can stop the barbarians," said the Conservative naively, "how can we hope to oppose it, especially since the few troops we have left will undoubtedly be on the Turtle's side?"

"It's perfectly obvious," declared the Secretary Royal. "The

Turtle never tires of protesting his unswerving loyalty to the Empire, its government, its laws, and its traditions. All we have to do is put an Emperor on the throne—any fool will do. The Turtle will have to recognize him, or else declare himself a revolutionary."

"You know. I think you've got something there. The only legal claim he has is the Emperor's will and his knightly title. We've already invalidated the will, and if the Turtle steps out of line, you could strip his title from him with one stroke of a gavel."

"Very well," said the Secretary Royal decisively.

"We have about a day and a half to fill that throne." The glint in his eyes reflected one part hope, one part resolution, and eight parts desperation as he turned back to the Round Table. The latest news had touched off a flurry of muttered consultations, which the Secretary Royal interrupted with violent blows of his rawhide mallet.

"Is there anyone here," he demanded," in favor of turning the imperial throne over to the Turtle?"

There was an ugly, decidedly negative, roar.

"There's an alternative," said the Secretary Royal, "a slim chance, but well worth striving for. An Emperor can be chosen from our own midst if he can poll a bare plurality, from at least one-third of those present and voting. That's fourteen votes. We have just thirty-six hours. In anyone in favor of trying it?"

This time the ayes had it, with deadly vengeance.

"The Imperial Hall of Kings," announced the Secretary Royal, "will now come to order. Nominations will be accepted for the perpetual and hereditary office of Emperor."

The forty-one delegates came to order, all at once, at the tops of their ragged voices.

TWENTY-FIVE

THE SCARECROW AND THE SAINT

Just north of the hamlet where the Citizens' Conservative Army had been founded and activated, the Scarecrow sat freezing by the almost deserted highway, waiting for the infrequent widow, old man, incorrigible subversive, or whomever else continued to flee south for one reason or another, instead of joining the Turtle's drive north. Since the Turtle had begun recruiting refugees, the begging trade downstream had fallen off sharply, and the Scarecrow lived mainly on acorns.

"I've lost her many times," he mourned, "and this anguished heart of mine could even bear to lose her many times again, but why, oh, why, was it Fate's design that I lose her to my worst and oldest enemy? After using men as pawns in her own game all her life, why must it be the Turtle with whom she finally falls so slavishly in love?"

It was now the dead of winter. The Scarecrow's laments condensed into vapor and streamed away on the biting wind. He had been waiting for hours for a possible benefactor to happen by, but no one came. His hands and feet were numb as stone. Although he was limp and feeble with hunger, he had to get up and stagger along the road to avoid freezing. His deadened feet and ankles behaved capriciously; he soon stumbled and fell into a snowbank. The snow was stingingly cold for the first minute or so, after which it began to feel strangely warm and soft. The Scarecrow made one perfunctory effort to get up again, then relaxed.

"I'll lie here and freeze," he decided. "There's no sense in standing up, even if I could. I'll never move again. I'll never hope for anything, or desire or fear or hate anything, ever again. Nothing can touch me. Already my arms and feet are numb. Soon the oblivion will spread to my brain and soul, and I'll be safe forever. Let this preposterous life of mine end here, for there's no hope left for the least of my dreams."

"Salve," greeted a mild voice.

"No!" screamed the Scarecrow. "Not you!"

"Arise, my son, for your destiny awaits you."

"No! Leave me alone. I beg you! What unspeakable crimes could I have committed to deserve even what I've already suffered? I've had too much of Destiny!"

"You must come with me," said the Saint, kindly but sorrowfully, "for you are not yet destined to die."

TWENTY-SIX

THE HALL OF KINGS

"According to the communique before me," said the Secretary-Royal, "the so-called Citizens' Conservative Army, poorly equipped, exhausted from a long march, outnumbered fifty to one, and fighting on foot against cavalry, has, by courage alone, won a decisive victory and thrown the barbarians into full disorderly retreat. The main body of the Turtle's rabble will pursue them as far as the northern frontier, where they will man the outposts until the Imperial Regulars can relieve them. His Potency and a small contingent are coming here to present a petition—the nature of which he does not disclose in all four pages of fine print."

The Secretary Royal laid the parchments on the table before him. "That means, gentlemen, that the Turtle is on his way here and will arrive any minute. I wish we could have chosen a successor to his Radiance, but it was too much to hope. I knew that, of course, before we started, but I had to try. You'll never know how happy I am that we've finally managed to agree on this one resolution...We are agreed, are we not, that we'll surrender the Imperial Citadel with good grace and refrain from making complete fools of ourselves?"

"A fat lot of choice we have," said a Theocrat bitterly.

"Most of us can count on being imprisoned as war criminals," added a Neutral. "But if we try to reason with him, he'll kill us all."

Heads nodded fatalistically around the Round Table.

"If only the Turtle had remained loyal," sighed a Conservative. "If he'd recruited a couple of new legions for the Imperial Regulars and promised them medals instead of titles...but what's done is done. I'll never trust a commoner again."

"If only it were a genuine people's army," contradicted a Radical, "instead of a gullible mob of turncoat proletarians, deluded by the Turtle's reactionary lies."

"I'd like to suggest once more," said the Secretary Royal," that the Turtle will probably recognize a legitimate Emperor, duly elected by the Hall of Kings. The most support any one candidate has received is eight votes; six more would give him a legal plurality as defined in the Great Charter. That candidate was a Neutral—no, excuse me—what do you call your party now?"

"It slips my mind," said the candidate glumly.

"Be that as it may, this man's eight ballots are the closest we have to a plurality. If I agree to change my vote and support him, in return for certain concessions, will five more of you do the same?"

"Aye!" cried the Neutrals.

"Nay!" cried the Radicals, Conservatives. Moderates, Liberals. Theocrats. Southern Gentlemen, Vegetarians, Omnivores, bandit chieftains, and independents.

"Then," said the Secretary Royal solemnly, "we have no choice but to surrender the Citadel, this last fragment of a once-great Empire. We have collectively chosen to accept defeat rather than compromise our respective principles. It's a decision I personally regret, but I have to admit there's a certain honor about it, almost a heroism. Let us now be true to this ideal, such as it is, and accept the consequences with dignity. No quibbling and no whining. Are we agreed?"

There was a ripple of fatalistic assent.

From beyond the heavy double doors of the Assembly Chamber, far off down the corridor, came the sound of drums and many sandals marching. The noise drew closer and grew louder until it seemed the conquerors must be right outside, and still, the volume increased. When the tramping and drumming were almost deafening, the drums gave a final roll and crash, and the marching footsteps halted.

Their ears were still ringing from the Turtle's impressive

approach. The delegates in the Hall watched the massive doors swing open. The first two guidon-bearers entered with the Turtle's pennon. As the Emperor's heir, the Turtle ought, by rights to have adopted the bearings of the imperial family, or at least differenced them, but, either out of pride in his own lineage or mere sentimental attachment for his vert snapping-turtle, he had merely quartered his escutcheon to make room for the Emperor's devices. Nor had he resisted the temptation of adding a crest, two supporters, and a scroll.

The guidon-bearers headed two columns of soldiers. With tight military precision, the columns divided and filed around either side of the Round Table. Two soldiers stopped and marked time behind each chair. Their captain barked a command, and they halted, all heels clicking simultaneously. At another command, they faced toward the Round Table, two behind each delegate, javelins at order arms. The delegates tensed and shrank deeper into their chairs.

Next, two heralds marched in, halted, sidestepped smartly to either side of the entrance, raised their coach-horns to their lips, and blew a long, complicated fanfare in close harmony. Then they lowered the horns and chanted, in perfect unison:

"Knight of the Old Order. General in temporary retirement of the Emperor's Own Troops, Founder and Supreme Commander of the Citizens' Conservative Army, Permanent Secretary of the Dynamic Feudalist Party, harasser of anarchists, slayer of barbarians, restorer of moral government and scourge of all wrong thinking: his Potency, THE TURTLE!"

The snare-drums rolled, and the Turtle himself entered. His armor was polished until it glittered blindingly. He had found a gold-plated helmet somewhere, which he carried on his arm. He marched up to the Round Table, set down his helmet, clicked his heels, and saluted the delegates in the Hall. His powerful voice rang out:

"If there be an Emperor at this time, then I request an audience with his Imperial Radiance. If, as I have heard, there is still no lawful Emperor upon the throne, then I address myself to your acting chairman."

The Secretary Royal weighed his words and answered.

"No worthy successor has yet been found for his late-lamented

Radiance. I have served as Secretary Royal for many years, and I believe I may still speak for this assembly, in spite of the changing times. We anticipated your arrival and have passed certain resolutions in preparation..."

His soul failed him here, for a moment. This was the culmination of a long, losing fight against chaos. Valiantly, he strove to maintain his outward composure in the face of ultimate disaster, for he was the last spokesman of the Old Order, and the Old Order had to fall with dignity and pride, as it had lived. He was the picture of tragic dignity as he continued.

"It is our studied conclusion that resistance to your coup will avail naught at this late date, either for the Empire or for ourselves; therefore, on behalf of the Imperial Government. I hereby surrender the Imperial Citadel to the Citizens' Conservative Army. We hope," he added reluctantly, only because it was his duty to do so, "that your Potency will respect the ancient customs of the Empire, and bear in mind that we, the delegates to the Hall of Kings, are of the royalty by legal definition, and thus as your prisoners are entitled to certain rights."

It was said. History was ended.

"On behalf of the Citizens' Conservative Army," replied the Turtle, "I gratefully thank your Majesties for the superlative hospitality of the Hall of Kings. However, if I may take the liberty of correcting an understandable misimpression, we have not come as irresponsible revolutionaries and certainly do not wish to go on record as having interrupted the Empire's long and glorious history by seizing the Hall of Kings. I cannot accept your Majesties' surrender.

We have come only to offer our services."

He had spoiled everything. The Secretary Royal gave him a look of frank hatred, but the Turtle seemed not to notice it.

"Indeed, your Majesty," the Turtle went on, "if this august body will merely agree to a few trivial conditions, the Citizens' Conservative Army will immediately merge with the Imperial Regulars. We shall formally pledge our allegiance to the Empire, the Great Charter, and the Hall of Kings, and undertake without delay to restore law and order throughout the forty-one provinces."

"This is a pleasant surprise," said the Secretary Royal boredly.

"We're most anxious to hear your conditions if you'll be so kind as to summarize them for us."

"Gladly, your Majesty, although they're so few and so simple, that they can hardly be described as conditions at all. They are, *primo*, that all imposters, who do not represent legitimate provincial governments, be removed from the Hall of Kings; *secundo*, that certain officers of the Citizens' Conservative Army, who have distinguished themselves in the service of the Empire, be awarded various aristocratic titles and fiefs, so chosen as to fill existing vacancies, and, *tertio*, that a successor to his late Radiance be crowned with no further delay, so that we may once again call ourselves an Empire, and not just another barbarian republic."

There was a pause.

"Is that all?" asked the Secretary Royal, who had been prepared to hear a much longer list of demands.

"That's all, your Majesty."

The Secretary Royal nodded. "I'm sure we can contrive to meet these very reasonable terms," he said, "but may I first inquire what plans your army has in case some of my honored colleagues find fault with the agreement?"

"In that case, your Majesty, the Citizen's Conservative Army will be forced—with very heavy hearts. I assure you—to resort to more direct means of rescuing the Empire from chaos. I'm sure it will be more satisfactory to everyone if we're allowed to merge with the Imperial Regulars."

"I see," said the Secretary Royal." Well, gentlemen, does his Potency's generous offer find unanimous acceptance, or is there anyone who feels it needs discussion?"

He looked around at the delegates. They, in turn, regarded the encircling soldiers. There was no discussion.

"There are a few details which I think could bear further clarification," said the Secretary Royal, seeing that the responsibility was his, "For example, it is your very worthy aim to rid all imposters from the Hall of Kings, but exactly how do you propose that we distinguish between impostors and legitimate delegates? Your Potency is doubtless aware that if the legality of each delegate's tenure is put to the vote, a few of us may be somewhat influenced by partisan prejudice."

"For the time being, let each delegate's conscience be his

guide," replied the Turtle. "Once there is an Emperor on the throne. I'm sure his Radiance will make short shrift of any imposters who remain."

The delegates eyed each other suspiciously.

"Good enough," said the Secretary Royal. "In the meantime, how will the worthy officers whom you propose as candidates for knighthood know whether they are knighted by a legitimate king or by an imposter?"

"As their commander," explained the Turtle, "I am responsible for safeguarding the legal rights of my legionaries. In the absence of a judge with better qualifications, I myself may have to decide who knights whom."

"It's what you might call killing one bird with two stones," the Secretary Royal philosophized. "Your selections will give added force to the dictates of our consciences. Concerning your third stipulation, you realize. I think that we've been trying for some months to elect an Emperor—since the heir was not on hand to claim his crown—and we have not yet found anyone who measures up to our standards. Since every candidate has already been rejected, perhaps you'd like to nominate someone yourself."

"I'd not be so presumptuous as all that," said the Turtle with a slight bow, "but if someone else deems me worthy. I should consider it my patriotic duty to answer the call and accept your nomination." He took a close look at his fingernails.

"That isn't exactly what I meant," said the Secretary Royal.

"I feared it wasn't, exactly," said the Turtle regretfully. "I'm aware that certain legislation—of undisputed constitutionality but doubtful justice—has more or less consigned me to the ranks of your 'rejected candidates.' This is the law of the land and cannot be lightly disregarded. Still, his Radiance's will did tend to favor me rather heavily, and I don't see why this wouldn't be tantamount to a nomination. Of course, the issue must be settled by due process, and I wouldn't want to exert pressure—other than to ensure justice by having my soldiers supervise the counting of the ballots."

"In death as in life," said the Secretary Royal, "His Radiance is out of order. According to the present, revised, Rules of Order, the Emperor may second nominations and other motions, but these motions must be introduced by the mere royalty. I'm afraid there's no way the Imperial will and testament can be construed as a nomination."

"I have a better suggestion," said another Conservative, "Why don't we just repeal the law that disenthroned the Turtle in the first place? Letting him have the title by direct succession will be much simpler and possibly less hazardous."

"Capital idea. I suppose," said the Secretary Royal. "I second the motion. All in favor?"

"Aye," said the author of the motion. No one else spoke.

"All in favor," said the Turtle pleasantly, "will signify by remaining in this building. Those opposed—" A Radical sprang up. "On what authority do you make the Rules of Order?" he demanded.

"It's one of my prerogatives as Emperor," said the Turtle.

"You're putting the cart before the horse!" the Radical accused.

"I'm a plain, blunt man, your Majesty," said the Turtle, "and metaphors often elude me, especially dead ones."

"There's nothing dead about that horse! You're trying to arrogate the Emperor's privilege of dictating the Rules of Order by which you hope to be chosen Emperor, not only before your coronation but before there are even valid Rules of Order by which to elect an Emperor. Your Majesties, I appeal to the Hall! Have we lost all concept of orderly legislative procedure?"

"Aye," said the Secretary Royal. "Some time ago."

"Majesties," said the Turtle reproachfully, "you speak as if this were a republic. In our Empire, the succession of heads of state is an orderly process, quite independent of passing revisions in the Rules of Order. However," he added magnanimously, "I will admit that his Majesty's point wasn't badly put." He turned to the Conservative, whose motion was under debate. "Your Majesty, would you be so kind as to amend your motion to make it retroactive by about ten minutes? I believe it would untangle this Radical Majesty's paradox."

"As your Radiance wishes," sighed the king.

There was a chorus of accusing murmurs.

"Excuse me," said another Conservative," but let's set the record straight. Are we to understand that you gentlemen are actually supporting this militarist upstart and his throng of aspiring commoners?"

"Let us put that another way," said the Secretary Royal. "Let us say, rather, that we're trying very hard to save the Empire. If this *coup d'etat* can be fobbed off on future historians as a legitimate succession to the throne, then the Empire will have survived its worst crisis. If you keep on carping, a thousand years of history could easily go down the drain." He turned to the scribes. "Strike that from the record," he said.

"Well, maybe so," said the dissident Conservative. "Thank heaven he's at least a knight...of sorts."

"Now, majesties," said the Secretary Royal, "if there's no one sufficiently opposed to this resolution to argue the point with his Potency and/or Radiance, then let's crown him Emperor and go home for the day. All in favor?"

No one left the Hall, and the motion was carried. Smiling broadly, the Turtle walked around to the raised throne and mounted it.

"Since we're all tired," he said generously, "and since I'm a man of simple tastes, we may dispense with the usual formalities of a coronation, if you wish."

He picked up the crown of Empire from the stand before the throne, upon which it had been gathering dust all during the inter-regnum. He looked it over appreciatively and tried it on. It was a perfect fit.

He turned to the Round Table. "Well, majesties?"

The Secretary Royal stood up, raised his right hand, and said resignedly, "Hail his Radiance, the Turtle."

Two other kings, both Conservatives, rose and repeated the salutation. The rest of the delegates, recognizing a fait accompli when they saw one, followed suit, except for the Radical who had challenged the Turtle before. He folded his arms, frowned, and remained seated.

"I'd greatly appreciate having the unanimous allegiance of the Empire's provinces," said the Turtle. "One can govern more effectively with the will of the governed,"

"No," said the Radical, "I abstain."

At a sign from the Turtle, the two soldiers behind the Radical's chair came to parade rest and gently prodded him with the tips of their javelins. The Radical resisted for a few jabs, then rose and saluted.

"Hail his de facto Radiance, the Turtle," he snapped and immediately sat down again.

"Gentlemen," said the Turtle, unfolding a sheaf of notes, "words fail me—I mean Us— (I mean We mean Us)—um—words fail Us, at this time, to express Our grateful appreciation for the confidence you have placed in Us in selecting Us for this signal honor. We thank you from the very cockles of Our heart for your unanimous support, and We sincerely hope We may prove worthy of the trust and equal to your expectations. A few of you. We suspect, are a little disturbed by the fact that one or two corners have been cut and some of the Empire's proud traditions neglected, as, for example, in cutting the coronation ceremony to the bone. Please believe Us when We assure you that We regret these expedients just as deeply as you do. We must be realistic, however. The Empire's machinery of government has been allowed to fall into a lamentable state of disrepair, and every ill-afforded moment we spend on formalities is another moment of strife and lawlessness in the provinces. We shall earnestly endeavor to set your minds at ease on this question—to prove, by Our every future action, that the steps We have taken have been solely in an effort to serve the Empire and our great civilization."

There was scattered listless applause.

"And now, gentlemen," said the Turtle, "as Our first official act. We want to make formal announcement of the steps We have taken to ensure the perpetuation of Our imperial lineage and prevent the recurrence of the recent strife. We'd like to introduce the most wonderful girl in the civilized world, your future Empress."

He stretched an arm toward the door.

"Gentlemen, my fiancée."

The lapse in pronoun usage was overlooked. All heads turned to watch the entrance. The two heralds raised their horns and sounded another stirring fanfare, then chorused:

"The fiancée of his Imperial Radiance—Miss Azaza!" Eyebrows were raised, for Azaza's name and fame were familiar to all the delegates, and her face, among other things, was well known to many Azaza entered, looking poised and sultry. She was ravishingly tricked out in silk, ermine, and diamonds. There was a stir of admiration. Azaza glanced appreciatively around at the near-barbarian splendor of the Hall of Kings, and a covetous gleam came into her mascaraed eyes as she estimated the cost of the magnificent silken tapestries and the solid platinum chandeliers. Escorted by two soldiers in silver helmets, she came to take her place beside the Turtle. As she mounted the dais and took the Turtle's hand, the delegates stood up and applauded, somewhat more vigorously than they had for the Turtle himself.

The Turtle directed that a chair be placed for Azaza beside the throne; Azaza sat down gracefully, aware that all eyes were upon her. The Tuttle took the throne, and the delegates settled back to their chairs.

"There are only one or two items of business which brook no delay," said the Turtle, adjusting the crown on his head, after which We intend to declare a holiday in honor of Our engagement. First, however, let us arrange for the prompt ennoblement of a number of officers of the Imperial Regular Army—as Our brave company will henceforth be called."

He produced a bulky scroll. "We have here a list of names, with present military rank and recommended titles to be conferred. They range, you'll notice, all the way from esquirehood right on up to full royalty, with a view to filling every existing vacancy in the aristocracy, with a few nobles left over to take charge of purely military fiefs in the Imperial Regular Army. To begin with, will someone kindly second the motion? We realize We can enact this into law by imperial decree, but We'd much rather have your sanction, for the record."

"Begging your Radiance's pardon," said the Secretary Royal, "but your Radiance is out of order. According to the Rules of Order, as amended by the degree of his late Radiance your predecessor, the Emperor may second a motion but may not initiate one. It's one of the checks and balances of a civilized government."

"Hmm," said the Turtle. "That could cause a lot of unnecessary complication and delay. What does the Great Charter have to say on the subject?"

"Hoping to spare the Rules of Order from further entropy this early in the dynasty," said the Secretary Royal.

"I'll make his Radiance's motion myself."

"Thank you," said the Turtle. "We second that."

"All in favor?" said the Secretary Royal. No one spoke. The

Turtle signaled to the soldiers, who prodded the delegates. There were muttered Ayes and some curses.

"All opposed?" said the Secretary Royal. Apparently, no one was opposed.

"Motion carried," said the Secretary Royal stoically, recording the fact in the Archives. The soldiers came back to attention. The Turtle handed the scroll to one of the orderlies in silver helmets, who carried it ceremoniously to the Secretary Royal. The Secretary Royal scanned it with evident distaste and passed it to a scribe, who filed it.

"We'd like to get just a few of the more important ennoblements out of the way today," said the Turtle, "Before that can be undertaken, however. We must first take steps to ensure that the honors are conferred by legitimate proxies of royalty." (The delegates began to fidget,) "And that, in turn, will require ridding this assembly—"

Half the double door of the Hall opened, and the Turtle paused in midsentence. The Saint entered.

"Well, father," exclaimed the Turtle. "To what may We attribute this unexpected honor?"

"Salvete," greeted the Saint blandly. "I have come to save the Empire from a great error which might otherwise have been made. Please forgive the disturbance, but it is necessary."

"Certainly," said the Emperor. "You're welcome any time. The floor is yours."

"First of all, my son, allow me to add my voice to the universal acclaim you so richly deserve for driving the heathen invaders from our land."

"I saw my duty, and I did it," said the Turtle modestly. "You might say it was all in a day's work."

"It was an act of unparalleled heroism," said the Saint. "But, alas, you are to be rewarded in other ways than this. The ways of Destiny are often obscure to poor mortals like ourselves, but we may know that behind the unfathomable complexity, there is a Plan and a Meaning. Heroes make themselves, my son, but Emperors are selected by the Universe. I have come to tell you of your true destiny, which until today I have not been allowed to disclose. It has been predestined from all time that you enter the Monastery of the Spina Mundi, there to study for the priesthood of the Established Faith."

Jaws dropped unanimously.

"Priesthood!" cried the Turtle. "Me? There must be some mistake, father. I'm a man of action. You know I'd never have the patience to achieve enlightenment."

The Saint spread his hands. "It is a universal law of Nature," he said, "that all men shall complete their lives in every phase, each to the limits of his inborn capacity. Truly, most men accomplish this merely by making a living, raising a family, and attending an occasional mass, but such a commonplace existence is not for you. You are destined for mightier things and in rich variety. Everything you have done has been done on a heroic scale, to be sure, but there are still vast, uncharted continents of your destiny which you have not yet touched and which you must explore minutely. Human beings err, but the Universe does not. There is no mistake, my son, for this is destined."

He finished and folded his arms in his sleeves. The Turtle took off the imperial crown to scratch his head, then sat tapping the bejeweled emblem on the arm of the throne. The Saint and the delegates waited while he made up his mind.

"Father," the Turtle said, "I believe you've given voice to my innermost thoughts—thoughts to which I've never paid any serious attention, after they first occurred to me, until this moment. Recently I suffered a lapse of memory, as you know, and during that time, with no mundane details to distract me. I did a great deal of thinking."

"That lapse of memory," said the Saint softly, "was arranged by Destiny, to give you the leisure to think, and to know your true self."

"I suppose it must have been. In any case, what you say is quite true, and it's been in the back of my mind for some time that my life hasn't been very well rounded. I've been a soldier most of my life, and I think I can say in all modesty that I've been a good soldier. I've also found time to do some reading, now and then, so I don't think my intellect has been entirely neglected. But, as you say, the spiritual side of my life has hardly been touched. I ought to do something about it."

"A wise resolve," said the Saint warmly.

Azaza looked worried. She got a grip on each arm of her chair, as though preparing to resist any attempt on the part of Fate to remove her from her Imperial Citadel.

"Thus ends the shortest dynasty in history," the Secretary Royal commented with disgust. "Ever since the Emperor passed away, we've been trying to get some kind of a successor on the throne. Now, five minutes after we get one crowned, he decides to retire from public life and study for the priesthood. Now we can start over again."

"Have no fear on that count," said the Turtle. "I won't retire without naming a successor."

"That will not be necessary," said the Saint helpfully. "As I indicated, Destiny has already selected a suitable Emperor."

"Whom'?" cried several delegates, hopefully.

The Saint smiled and turned to the half-open door. Trying to shrink invisibly into his ragged scholar's robe, the Scarecrow edged nervously into the assembly chamber.

"This," said the Saint, "is the man whom the all-wise and all-knowing Universe has destined to be your Emperor."

For a few horrifying seconds, there was dead silence, while everyone gaped at the Scarecrow, and the Scarecrow looked fearfully from face to face, overcome with stage-fright. Then the Turtle gave a bellow, and Azaza gave a scream, and the delegates of one accord leaped to their feet, shouting.

"I know him!" cried a Neutral. "He's a lunatic and a Radical to boot!"

"That's a lie!" yelled a Radical. "We don't claim him! We don't want him!"

"He's a chymist!" shouted a Theocrat, "a delver into forbidden knowledge! A dirty atheist!"

"A military upstart I can be forced to accept!" cried a Conservative, "but an egghead—never!"

"Throw him out!" shrilled Azaza. "Please, somebody, throw him out!"

Hearing Azaza's voice, the Scarecrow raised his unkempt head and spotted her in the crowd. In a split second, he was transformed from a cringing beggar into his old expressive self. With a piercing cry, he rushed to the Round Table, leaped to the huge tabletop, and dashed across to the far edge.

"My love!" he yelled, gesticulating wildly, "my light, my soul, my Azaza, to whom this anguished heart is eternally devoted! At last, I have something to offer you! At long last, I have a fitting gift to lay at your feet! How can I blame you for spurning me when I was a penniless scholar, for piercing my lovelorn heart with the cruel sting of your indifference until it burst asunder and flooded the entire province with the raging torrent of my tears? If you'll but relent, my beloved, my black despair will be transmuted into ecstatic joy, the livid scars of my grief will be healed without a trace, the shattered chalice of my heart will be made whole and will brim once more with rapture! Dearest Azaza, accept my bid for the fulfillment of all my fondest dreams, and be my Empress!"

Although this appeal was delivered in an earsplitting yell, it was almost drowned out by the babble of angry shouts from around the Round Table.

"Peace," begged the Saint, raising his hand, "please." A hush fell abruptly over the Hall of Kings. The Scarecrow gesticulated but had to stop when no words came forth. The delegates waved their fists and opened and closed their mouths but could not pierce the unnatural silence. One by one, they gave up and dropped back to their chairs.

The Saint solemnly circumvented the Round Table and mounted the dais to stand by the throne. The Turtle fatalistically handed him the imperial crown and stood down. He went to hold Azaza's hand, for she was looking terrified.

"Come, my son," said the Saint to the Scarecrow. "Take the throne of Empire for which you have been destined and receive the homage of the Hall of Kings."

Uncertainly, now that his moment had come, the Scarecrow climbed off the Round Table and shuffled to the throne. The Saint gestured him to the satin upholstery. The Scarecrow sat down cautiously on the edge of the throne, clutching nervously at the carved ivory arms. His tattered robe contrasted sharply with the backdrop of purple velvet. Everyone watched aghast, as spectators watch a grisly mishap at the chariot-races, while the Saint placed the crown on the Scarecrow's uncombed head. It was too large for him and dropped to his eyebrows.

The Saint turned to the stunned delegates. "Hail," he said. "Hail his Radiance the Scarecrow."

Torn with reluctance but driven by a compulsion sent from the dawn of eternity, the delegates rose, quivering in every muscle, suffering in every nerve, they raised their right hands.

"Hail..." they recited in choked voices, "...his Radiance,...the Scarecrow." Then they sank back to their chairs, defeated by a Power beyond mortal comprehension. The Secretary Royal broke down and sobbed.

"Your reign will be long and prosperous, your Radiance," the Saint prophesied.

"Father," protested the Secretary Royal, "a saint knows everything; you must know what I've suffered all these months, as I strove against insurmountable odds to restore sanity to a distraught government. How can you so callously drag his ex-Radiance away before he's had a chance to establish order? With the Empire still reeling, you've dashed its last hope by placing a Radical Emperor on the throne! Human civilization can't possibly survive this last and foulest blow! Is the Turtle's heroic campaign against the barbarians to be made a farce? Are my thirty years of service in the Hall to be a useless gesture, along with the efforts of all these delegates—who mean well in their sundry misguided ways? I can't believe that anyone, let alone a saint, could be so void of common decency!"

The Saint sighed, "Since I am not permitted to know—much less reveal—the ultimate Plan of Destiny," he said, "I can only assure your majesty that since the downfall of the civilization we know has occurred by the will of the Universe, it must be for the Highest Good thereof.

We must not place undue emphasis on our petty human aspirations when the welfare of all the Cosmos is involved, You and I are powerless to alter the Empire's predestined future, but we must have faith in the infinite wisdom of the Universe."

"That may be Fate," howled the Secretary Royal, "but don't ask me to accept it! I'll fight for order to my dying gasp! When death overtakes me. I swear I'll be pounding a gavel!"

"Your enterprise has the blessing of All There Is," said the Saint soothingly. "Your struggle for order. however futile, is your destined place in the fabric of existence."

"Father," said the Turtle, "I'd like to ask you about one thing before it's too late."

"Of course, my son."

"Before I commit myself to the career you've suggested, is it respectable for a holy man to marry? There's been some controversy lately. I understand, and I want to make sure it would be permissible in my case. Before I learned of my real work in life, you see, I fell in love."

"It is true that there is controversy," replied the Saint, "and until there is a definitive revelation on the subject, the Church has seen fit to leave such temporal decisions to individual discretion. Since spiritual understanding is enhanced by dissociation from worldly attachments, many priests remain single. On the other hand, if one is young and virile, and the unsated appetites of the flesh are likely to be a source of distraction, then it is often wisest to take a wife. There is ample precedent for either mode of existence."

The Turtle looked much relieved. He turned to Azaza.

"I trust, dearest, that my decision to follow a course of greater wisdom hasn't altered your affections."

"I—I'm rather confused," said Azaza.

"Don't listen to him!" shrieked the Scarecrow, flying from the throne and falling to his knees by Azaza's chair. "How could you believe that he loves you a tenth as much as I do? My love is as dedicated as the howling blizzard, as passionate as the charging elephant, as vast and deep as the universe, and as steadfast as the Spina Mundi! Marry me, beloved Azaza, and bring comfort to these bleeding shreds of a torn and lacerated heart!"

"My dear," said the Turtle, "although I can no longer offer you an Empire, still I can and do offer you myself and my undying affection. Don't be upset by the loss of these worldly vanities." He waved a deprecatory hand at the lush trappings of the Hall. "Come with me, my dear. Let us be on our way to seek the spiritual life —together."

Azaza still seemed a little confused. She looked at the Turtle, then at the Scarecrow. She looked sadly at the silken tapestries, the heavy platinum chandeliers, the thick Persian carpeting, and the ivory throne hung with purple velvet. She looked again at the Scarecrow in his gem-encrusted crown and winced. She looked at the Turtle in his polished steel armor.

She took a deep breath, "I'm really terribly sorry, sir," she said," for I was quite fond of you, but to decline a proposal from his Imperial Radiance would be...an act of treason;"

There was another startled silence. The Turtle's face was a mask of outrage. The Scarecrow's face was aglow with unbelieving joy. Neither suitor could collect his thoughts to speak. Finally, the delegates began to snicker, then to laugh. The Saint raised his hand and silenced them.

"My child," the Saint said to Azaza, "your decision is fully in accord with Destiny's plans for you, and I have already arranged for your wedding. It will be tomorrow morning in the Temple of the Macrocosm. His Saintliness the Prime Ecclesiarch will officiate. Blessings upon you both.?

"Come," he told the Turtle, "we must be on our way, for our destiny lies elsewhere."

The Turtle closed his mouth, blinked, turned with a jerk, and started resolutely for the door. He stopped, and came back to pick up his helmet, then made his exit. The Saint followed him out of the Hall, pausing to bless the assembly before the great doors closed behind him.

In transports of joy, the Scarecrow seized Azaza's hand and kissed it. Azaza gave a violent shudder but submitted bravely.

TWENTY-SEVEN

THE PATRIARCH

The Patriarch of Kalopolis sat at the table in his library, where he had been for most of the week. One end of the massive table was piled high with books; the other end was covered solidly with bottles. Overwork and discouragement had found room on the Patriarch's weathered visage for more lines than ever, and his eyes were sparks of desperation in cavernous hollows of weariness. He held a volume of Scripture in one hand and his goblet in the other.

Melli entered and began to gather up empty bottles. The Patriarch looked up from his book and shook his head sadly. His sunken eyes were terrible to behold.

"So little time left," he creaked, "and scores of sacred bottles—I mean books—I haven't opened yet." He leaned back in his chair and closed his aching eyes to give them a moment's rest. Melli picked up a flask and emptied the remaining drops into the Patriarch's cup. The Patriarch returned with a soft groan to his research.

"Never let it be said the Patriarch of Kalopolis ever gave up before he was beaten," he rasped, turning a page.

As she left, Melli glanced back at the Patriarch, glued studiously to his book as though some avenging deity with a pathological sense of poetic justice had doomed him to read forever on the same grueling schedule. Melli knit her brows sympathetically and left the room. As always, she kept her thoughts to herself.

Hours passed. The only sounds in the room were the whisper of pages turning. Late in the afternoon, when the daylight was giving out, the Patriarch's eyes suddenly widened, and he leaned closer to the page.

"Eh?" he said; "What's this?"

He snapped his fingers and reached for volume V of the Book of Prophesy. He riffled through it until he found the verse he thought he remembered seeing and compared it carefully with a passage in the Book of Truth.

"That's incredible!" he said. He opened volume II of the Book of Aphorisms.

"Aha?" he said, jotting down some cross-references. He rose with an excited crackling of joints and hobbled to the bookcase. He brought two more heavy volumes back to the table and hunted through volume XVII of the Book of Revelation.

"So," he said and wrote down some more page numbers. He leafed back to re-read some verses from volume I of the Book of Truth.

"Well, bless my soul!" he said. He made another trip to the bookcase and staggered back with volumes III, IV, XI, and XIX of the Book of Prophesy. He read first from volume III. His face lit up.

"Ho ho!" he said." This will curl that kid's whiskers!" He opened volume XIX to the next reference.

"Et tu, Melli," he said tragically. "Prophesies for everybody today—me, Melli, my disciple, the Scarecrow...I've struck it rich, haven't I?"

Next in order was volume IV. He eagerly ferreted out the cross-reference.

"An accomplice!" he exclaimed. "I should have realized Destiny wouldn't assign a job like this to a kid his age. I'm getting closer now. Here's the man I've got to find: 'One,' (it says here) '*whilk hath unscrupulouslie abvsed a position of priestlie responsibilitie to passe hys dayes in indolense, venerie & excesse'*

Obviously, an unstable type. It makes you wonder how he got into the priesthood in the first place. Now, who do I know who would fit that description?"

He rubbed his forehead in thought. In search of additional clues, he opened volume XI of the Book of Prophesy and sleuthed down a reference from his list. His eyes widened farther. "Why, this doesn't check!" he cried. "It's an out-and-out contradiction! If this isn't a printer's error, it could undermine our whole..."

Suddenly curious, he marked his place and turned back to finish reading the previous excerpt.

"Let me see now...'—*to passe hys dayes in indolence, venerie & excesse, fore it shalle come to passe that when this contemptyble wretche shalle tvrne to paige lxxii in ye XIth Booke of Prophesie, he shalle finallie & totallie destroye ye Chvrche bye that whilk he shalle reade therein."*

The Patriarch blanched. "Give me strength!" he croaked, uncorking a bottle.

TWENTY-EIGHT

THE SAINT AND THE TURTLE

"About fifteen minutes up the road," said the Turtle, peering ahead through the blowing mist, "is the fork where we parted company. You know, it's a good thing you saints keep most of your knowledge to yourselves. If you had told me everything that was in store, I think I'd have turned around and gone back to the farm."

"It is wrong to wish to change the Plan," said the Saint.

"I know," said the Turtle listlessly. "I had a destiny to fulfill, and it couldn't have been otherwise. Still, it makes you think."

"It can be most instructive," said the Saint, "to consider a past situation in the light of what has since developed. When you have become enlightened, you will be able to view the present and the future from the same superior perspective."

"That ought to be interesting," said the Turtle without enthusiasm. "I wonder how I'll ever get used to it."

"You will, my son. Many laymen wonder how we saints can bear to know the future, but there is really no difficulty, for such foresight comes only with complete reconciliation to Destiny."

"Maybe so," said the Turtle. "Anyway, if it's destined. I guess I'll give it the old try—it's not as though I might fail."

"Wisely spoken, my son," the Saint commended.

They walked on in silence for a few minutes, contemplating the future, each in his own way.

"There's something I don't quite understand," said the Turtle. "You told me I'd only be able to change my mind twice a year, on the solstices; yet apparently I was fated to resign as Supreme Commander of the Imperial Regulars, and then, later on, to step down as Emperor. I didn't think much about these things when they happened, but, looking back, have I missed a technical definition somewhere?"

"These apparent anomalies are easily explained," said the Saint. "On the first occasion, when you resigned your military command, it was not a change of mind, but an adaptation to changing circumstances, which is quite permissible even in Cosmic terms. Then, yesterday, when you decided to retire from public life altogether, it was the Winter Solstice."

"Oh, was it?" I must have lost track of the date."

The Saint nodded. "Amnesiacs often do," he said.

The Turtle did not answer.

TWENTY-NINE

THE PATRIARCH

His work finished, the Patriarch of Kalopolis sat staring out the window at the gathering dusk. A tear slid over his cheek, "Poor Church," he sighed, "Poor old Established Faith. Well, we tried."

He was about to ring for Melli, but she appeared just then, bringing a taper to light the lamp.

"I've solved the case," the Patriarch announced. "It didn't turn out the way I hoped, but so runs the world's luck, and at least it's settled now. It was all right there in the Scripture once I found the key."

Melli looked pleased and interested. She noticed that the Patriarch's appearance had improved vastly. His brow was clear again, or as clear as was normal for a man of his years.

"There had to be a mistake somewhere in the Plan," the Patriarch elaborated, "Sure enough, there were several. For one thing, that hare-brained kid got the prophecies mixed up. He instigated the right cataclysm—he had to; Destiny wouldn't have tolerated an anomaly of that magnitude—but the one he had in mind was the veritable grandma of all cataclysms, and actually, it wasn't due for ninety-four years. Didn't I always say he was a saint among saints? If events almost a century off look like the immediate future to his insight, just think what he could do in the oracular field—under responsible supervision, of course. He and I could write a supplement to the Book of Prophesy that would cover the next three thousand years! Well, now he thinks he's destroyed the Empire, and actually, he's just patched up a few of its weaknesses. Him and his pious drivel about never prying too deeply into the Plan! He sure had me coming and going; blast him! Let that be a lesson to you. Melli: never trust a man who takes religion too seriously."

Melli shook her head.

"Smart girl," agreed the Patriarch. Anyway, this cataclysm wasn't the big one, and it's almost blown over now. The real dilly of a cataclysm will hit us in ninety-four years. There has to be a competent Emperor on the throne to pull civilization through, and the purpose of this shake-up was to put one there. It might seem that one of the Turtle's descendants would be a good bet; I thought so myself until the Turtle abdicated in favor of the Scarecrow. What I didn't notice is that the Turtle's just a genetic fluke, and his offspring will regress toward the average. Destiny. Which sees all things, put the Scarecrow in power instead. Hard to fathom, isn't it?"

Melli nodded.

"It had me stumped, too, till I found the scriptural explanation today. The ways of Destiny are enigmatic, as my boy's so fond of reminding people. There's madness in the method, but there's a method. Azaza's no pillar of virtue, but she'll straighten up in a hurry, now that she's Empress. The Scarecrow's a lunatic, especially in his political views, but politics is just a passing interest to him. He'll get sick of power in a few weeks and go back to alchemy, and all the governmental responsibility will revert to the Hall of Kings. The Secretary Royal is destined to pull out of his current state of shock shortly and get busy filling up the Hall with good, solid, right-thinking Dynamic Feudalists from the Turtle's list. All the preparatory legislation was bulldozed through under the Turtle's administration, and his soldiers are still swarming all over the Imperial Citadel, making themselves hard to ignore as a pressure-group. The real meat of the matter, though, is that neither Azaza's morals nor the Scarecrow's radicalism has a thing to do with genetics. Azaza will bear him a son, the second Emperor of the new dynasty, who'll inherit the Scarecrow's brains and energy and Azaza's sound business sense. This combination of rare gifts will be transmitted through sixteen generations of wise, far-sighted, and responsible rulers before the line runs out; Destiny, using my disciple as an instrument, has arranged for several more centuries of civilization. It's confusing, on the face of things, but the Universe knows what It's doing."

The Patriarch tapped his forehead and winked. "Verily I say unto you. Melli, you have to be pretty sharp to put anything over on the Universe. I didn't quite make the grade, myself. After all that work, the joke's ultimately on me. While I was trying so hard to keep my disciple from destroying the Church, I destroyed it myself. It wasn't his destined mission at all, and now that I think about it, he never said it was."

Melli's eyes widened.

"That's right," the Patriarch insisted, "All this time, the villain was none other than me. While I was looking for a detailed prophesy of the Cataclysm in the Scripture, what to my wondering eyes should appear but a fatal flaw in our theology, just the sort of internal contradiction we've always prided ourselves on having eliminated. I traced it through, and there it was, spread all through the Scripture. There's been room for a few mistakes, after all, in three hundred forty-five volumes.

If our doctrines are self-contradictory, then logic forces us to scrap them all and start over. Then, to top it all off, I found a chapter in the Book of Prophesy that foretold my meddling six hundred years ago. That particular prophet obviously made a studied effort to overlook my finer qualities. I can forgive him most of his comments; his standards were old-fashioned, and I'd hardly expect him to heap blessings on the destroyer of the Church. What galls me is, he had the nerve to call me indolent! Just because I have my see running like clockwork and don't have to pay any attention to it, does that justify calling me lazy?"

Melli shook her head.

"For fifty years, I work my fingers to the bone for the Church, and then the Scripture calls me indolent! Think of the time and effort I've had to put in just to debunk the Scripture! Indolent indeed! Well. I've settled the score with that prophet. The Established Faith is finished, and he goes with it—nothing he ever said or wrote has any more claim to infallibility."

The Patriarch stood up, rubbing his hands. "The next thing," he said, "is to teach my disciple a lesson. I've run across a couple of prophecies about him, too, that should make his hair stand on end."

Chuckling wickedly, the Patriarch limped to the bookcase and began searching through the titles in his matchless collection of pornography. "Destiny's full of surprises," he went on, "and some of them are tough to take if you're not enlightened. Take the Scarecrow: if he'd been a saint, he wouldn't have been so broken up by losing his invention to the Neutrals, would he? How was the poor fellow to know the Figure had to fall into the Neutrals' hands because they were the only faction that would have kept it here in Kalopolis, as Destiny intended?"

He selected a book and took out a small brass key he had hidden between the leaves. He replaced the book on the shelf and limped over to the Chinese cabinet.

"The Figure had to stay in Kalopolis, to keep peace and quiet in this region so I could work without being interrupted by barbarian invaders. Without the Scarecrow's misfortunes, the Church couldn't have been destroyed as destined. The Scarecrow could have taken all his setbacks more philosophically if he'd been enlightened, but then he wouldn't have been an alchemist, so he couldn't have built the Figure in the first place."

He unlocked a drawer in the cabinet. "I want you to run one more errand for me. Melli," he said as he rummaged through the drawer. "I know it's after dark, but it would take several days if I sent any other messenger, and you've got to catch my disciple before either he or the Turtle commits himself to anything. They're on their way to the mountains—you know where the pass is. I want you to catch up with my disciple and give him something."

He shook the drawer impatiently. "If I can find it, that is. Watch his face when you hand it to him. It'll call his spiritual attention to something he's never thought of before. Ha! I wish I could be there...unless the Prime Ecclesiarch's already told him. That's the trouble with his Saintliness—he's too damned holy; he knows too much. If he's beat me to it, the surprise is ruined."

The Patriarch poured the contents of the drawer out on top of the cabinet and raked through the assortment with his fingers. "I don't think he told him anything, though, because if he had, my disciple would be on his way here instead of to the monastery, and the Scripture prophesies that he's headed for the monastery. That's one virtue I'll give old Lardguts credit for—he minds his own business. He knows enough about Destiny to leave It alone. He's done a creditable job of leaving me alone too, all these years, blinking some of my less saintly habits. He knew how all this was destined to turn out, and he knew if I'd been any holier than I am, the Church might have been destroyed fifty years too soon. For another thing, he knew better than to read certain parts of the Scripture—the passages I found today! Ah, here it is."

The Patriarch turned back to Melli. "Here; give this to my disciple and watch his eyes pop open. Go like the wind, because there's not much time. The boy will be preaching to the Turtle, and it's important that the Turtle doesn't commit himself any farther than he already has."

Melli held up a forefinger. "Yes?" said the Patriarch.

Melli indicated the bookcase full of Scripture and cocked her head questioningly.

"Oh, the Church?" said the Patriarch. "Don't worry about it— I'll take care of everything. I found some flaws in the logical structure of our theology, and people don't tolerate defects like that in religion nowadays—but it's nothing that can't be doctored up. It'll mean rewriting the Scripture from end to end, perhaps adding a few dozen volumes, but that's nothing—our Scripture's been revised many times. Of course, the Established Faith is finished as such; we'll have to change the name—call it the Reformed Established Faith, or something imaginative like that. I won't have to worry about unemployment, though. I'm getting too old to be a patriarch anyway, and I need something more sedentary. Rewriting the Scripture will be a good job for my declining years."

Melli nodded understandingly.

"You'd better get going," said the Patriarch, "and this time I really mean it. You haven't got more than five minutes to get there."

Melli nodded again and obediently vanished. The doorcurtains billowed and flapped in her slipstream. There was a roar of wind in the courtyard as she departed.

"*Quam puella!*" chuckled the Patriarch fondly. He sat down at the table and poured wine. "The fastest *puella* in Kalopolis. How will I ever get along without her? But it's destined. At least it's in the Scripture that she'll leave me in another six months, and not in any of the chapters I have to revise, so I guess it's destined."

He tossed off a drink and sighed resignedly, "*Nubat illa, et morbus effugiet*. I wonder how she'd have reacted if I'd been allowed to tell her she's destined to meet her beau for the first time tonight."

He poured another drink and drank it.

"It's for the best, after all. Her life with me hasn't been ideal from that standpoint—I'm not the man I was sixty years ago."

THIRTY

MELLISUGA-HELENAE

The mountain mist had thickened into a cold drizzle, and somewhere behind it, the sun had set. A damp wind sprang up. The Saint pulled his hood up against the chill. The Turtle was still in armor, better protected from javelins than from weather. He wished he still had the woolen habit he had discarded at the inn when he recovered his memory and resumed his normal identity. This made him think of the reunion with Azaza and of the ill-starred romance which had followed.

"I trust you are reconciled to parting from your beloved," said the Saint, almost as if he were reading the Turtle's thoughts. "She was not destined for you, you know."

The Turtle snorted. "Nor I for her! Reconciled is hardly the word—I can't understand what attracted me to such a woman in the first place, except, of course, that it must have been destined. No, father, my only real regret is at having to leave the government in the hands of a Radical Emperor. I'm sure I could have saved civilization, even from the state it's in, but the Scarecrow will never be able to restore order among the provinces. I don't pretend to be a prophet, yet, but certainly, the future can hold nothing but decades of civil strife and probably another barbarian invasion. Thousands of people will die needlessly."

"You have an unwholesome attitude toward death," the Saint

chided mildly. "When you are enlightened, you will see how meaningless it is to view death as a misfortune. Think of it as release from the oppressive yoke of mortal striving, and deliverance to oblivion's blessed repose."

"I'll try," said the Turtle, "but it's not easy to change so many mental habits all at once.

I guess you know that; you've been through it all. Look, there's our fork in the road, and isn't that a light I see up there, through the fog?"

"We are not destined to meet anyone until we arrive at the monastery tomorrow afternoon," said the Saint factually, without looking up.

"My imagination. I guess," mumbled the Turtle.

They climbed on toward the fork. The Turtle peered ahead, trying to convince himself there was no one there. The closer they came, however, the more vivid the illusion became. At last, it took the unmistakable form of a girl in a scarf and a heavy cloak, holding a lantern.

The Saint finally looked up and stopped in his tracks. His mouth opened. "Why, this is impossible!" he gasped. "This was not destined!"

The Turtle was also surprised at meeting another human being in the Spina Mundi, but even more surprised to learn that something could surprise the Saint.

"Hello," the Turtle called. "Who Goes There?"

Melli approached the two travelers, moving at a normal speed so that she would not startle them. She went to the Saint, nodded in greeting, and handed him something small and triangular. The Saint examined it in wonder.

It was a guitar pick.

The Turtle studied Melli's face, but it was mostly hidden by her hood and scarf.

"I don't believe I've had the pleasure of meeting you, have I?" he inquired.

Melli smiled fleetingly and shook her head.

The Turtle hesitated, then looked to the Saint for an introduction. The Saint was standing with his eyes closed, holding the guitar pick on his open palm. Not wishing to disturb his meditation, the Turtle turned back to Melli.

"Allow me to introduce myself," he said. "I'm called the Turtle."

Melli bobbed her head politely and still said nothing.

The Turtle hesitated again. "You...ah...don't talk to strangers?" he ventured.

Melli shook her head apologetically. "Oh," said the Turtle. "I see."

The Saint came to his rescue without opening his eyes. "Her name is Mellisuga-helenae," he said. "She is a servant in the household of my venerable teacher."

"Honored. I'm sure," said the Turtle. "Your name interests me; I seem to recall having read it somewhere. Isn't 'Mellisuga-helenae' a naturalists' term for a species of hummingbird?"

Melli nodded brightly.

"That's a very pretty name," said the Turtle. Melli smiled and blushed slightly.

"Do you live around here?" the Turtle inquired conversationally. "I didn't realize there was any settlement at all, in this part of the Empire."

Melli shook her head and pointed along the road south.

"Kalopolis?" said the Turtle incredulously. "You're a long way from home. What brings you to a place like this, at this hour, in mid-winter?"

Melli nodded toward the Saint.

"She came to bring me a message," said the Saint, "from my teacher, the Patriarch of Kalopolis, a wise and holy man—" He bowed his head and put one hand to his brow. "—just how wise and how holy I have only now come to realize."

"Is something wrong, father?" asked the Turtle.

"Much has been revealed to me," said the Saint dolefully. He opened his eyes, which were full of tragedy. "The deeper wisdom which has come to me has greatly altered circumstances.

I cannot go with you to the mountains, my son, for I have urgent business in Kalopolis."

"Oh?" Not bad news. I hope."

"Bad news," the Saint confirmed, "very grave indeed. My teacher has sent me this—" He displayed the guitar pick. "—to call my attention to a terrible oversight." He sighed forlornly. "And yet this, too, was destined since the beginning of time. Strange are the ways of Destiny. Which sometimes hides the Truth even from Its saints. I myself am to blame, of course—insofar as a mere mortal can be held accountable." His voice took on a dreamy quality as he mentally explored the implications of his new insight.

"But father," the Turtle protested, "I thought saints knew everything."

The Saint shook his head slowly. "No, alas! We who have attained enlightenment can know anything, but not everything; only the Universe knows All. We saints know only what we happen to think about, and our minds are finite—as I have just been reminded to my sorrow."

"I'm sorry to hear it," said the Turtle, "but I'm afraid I don't quite understand what you mean."

"My oversight," the Saint explained, "has led to a frightful anomaly in the Plan of Destiny, which it has taken a greater and more virtuous man than myself to correct. My venerable teacher— whom in my pride and ignorance I thought I had surpassed in spiritual excellence—still has many things to teach me. That, in essence, was my oversight."

He turned to Melli. "Return, child, and let my honored teacher know I have received his message, and that of the Universe. I am humbled and repentant, and I shall return immediately to Kalopolis to resume my neglected education."

Melli nodded respectfully. She darted one brief, coy glance at the Turtle, and then she was gone in a swirl of fog. The Turtle stared thoughtfully in the direction she had gone.

After a few seconds, he blinked and turned back to the Saint.

"What do you suggest?" he asked. "If you go back to Kalopolis, I'll have no teacher, but I can't change my plans to study theology."

"You must go on alone, my son. I am not worthy of teaching you, for I have learned that my own enlightenment has barely begun. There will be others at the monastery much better qualified than I to guide you on the Singlefold Path."

"If it's destined," said the Turtle realistically, "then I guess we don't have much choice. I hope you'll do me one favor, though: begin my instruction now by letting me share this great truth you've just perceived. If it's the sort of mistake, a man like you can make. I doubt that I could avoid it on my own."

"It cannot be expressed in words," replied the Saint sadly. "It is spiritual Truth, which you must discover for yourself through enlightenment. Return to the world of human beings when you have found it."

"I suppose so," said the Turtle ambiguously.

The Saint raised his eyes devoutly to the dark, lowering sky. "All is well," he murmured. "Not even my flagitious error could appreciably alter the course of Destiny, for my teacher has already repaired the damage I have done. Be cheered to know that spirituality, in a higher and truer form than ever before, has been preserved for mankind. This much, at least. I am permitted to reveal."

He smiled beatifically at the Turtle. "How far-reaching was the wisdom of my mentor," he said reverently, "who has saved my guitar for me all these years."

"I'm still not sure I understand," said the Turtle with a trace of impatience.

"No," the Saint agreed, "but you will see someday when you have attained enlightenment. And now farewell. Go in peace, my son, and the blessings of All There Is be with you."

The Saint took the same road as before, toward Kalopolis, while the Turtle stood scratching his head, as before. The Saint paused and turned. He made a sign of benediction, then went on.

When the fog had swallowed the Saint, the Turtle sat down on a convenient boulder, crossed his legs, rested his chin on his fist in the manner of Le Penseur, and did some deep, serious thinking. He sat there, thinking, for a long time, until twilight had thickened almost into night.

After a while, he extracted a tablet and stylus from his helmet and wrote: MELLISUGA HELENAE, and then: HIS REV. THE PTCH.OF KLPS.

He put the tablet away, put the helmet back on his head, stood up, hoisted his duffle bag back onto his shoulder, and resumed his journey.

"Destiny is full of twists," he mused profoundly. "One can hardly blame us laymen for suspecting that the Universe is insensate, sometimes. I've learned at least that a mere mortal is ill-advised to shirk a clear-cut destiny. Still and all, something tells me I'm cut out for a more active career than the priesthood. From now till the Summer Solstice should be ample time to grasp the fundamentals of theology, and I wonder why the fundamentals wouldn't be sufficient, even for a man with a destiny like mine."

Far away up the canyon, a griffin shrieked. The Turtle stopped and listened, frowning and fingering the hilt of his sword. There was a long silence.

Suddenly the Turtle's frown faded, and his eyebrows shot up in astonishment. Snare drums! His own snare drums! He had almost forgotten about them.

"Yes, definitely," he decided. "I have six months to think of a suitable career, though I'd probably be wisest to wait till I get to Kalopolis before I make any definite plans. Plans aren't always easy to change—that's another important lesson of my life."

The griffin screamed again, a little closer than before, but the sound of drumbeats was louder, too. A vulture, startled by the martial rattling, rose from its perch on some animal's weathered skeleton and flapped angrily up out of earshot. The Turtle walked on, absorbed with visions of the future.

"How different that girl is from Azaza," he said. "She has a strange, quiet beauty that's all her own—and her conversation is perfectly enchanting. His Reverence the Patriarch must be a man of excellent taste. I'll enjoy meeting him, too."

Briskly whistling his favorite march, he strode on up the trail through the blowing mist.

FINIS

ACKNOWLEDGMENTS

This is the second major work by Jon. P. Gunn. I originally met Jon P. Gunn through a Navy friend in 1983. He inspired me, entertained me, challenged me and then finally gave me one of the greatest gifts that I ever received, the manuscript for The Apes of Eden. He died shortly thereafter but made a solemn last request that I wait 30 years before sharing the Apes with the world. I have honoring that request by publishing The Apes of Eden.

iCrew Digital Productions started as a high school club at Hilltop High consisting of very talented individuals who are just now reaching the primes of their careers. iCrew was preceded by another group of students equally talented as a part of Southwest High Video Productions. iCrew continues with young, talented group of photographers at Mater Dei Catholic High School in Chula Vista. These kids are my inspiration and my family. iCrew continues as our members grow and as iCrew Digital Publishing.

iCrew Member Karin Street has provided much needed business sense and advice. Thanks to DJ Rogers for her string of great covers. Thanks go to Jim Bennett for his kind reviews and his editing suggestions.

And my greatest thanks to the author, who continues to inspire me. Each time I read Gunn's books, I learn more about him and his wonderful legacy. He was a magician with words. Let the magic continue.

ABOUT THE AUTHOR

Jon P. Gunn completed The Saint and the Turtle when he was thirteen years old. He read Spenser, Chaucer, Dante and Cervantes.

Jon never graduated from college even though he had twice the number of hours to graduate. He was too busy reading the great works of literature to bother. He is survived by a single child. It is that man and his friend, Rick Lakin who are bringing you Jon's work. We think it's very good. We hope you do too.

Website for The Apes of Eden

ISBN: 978-1-946739-13-1

This is a work of fiction and all characters and events mentioned are imaginary.
Printed in the United States of America
Published by iCrew Digital Publishing
Website: icrewdigitalpublishing.com
e-mail: icrewdigital@gmail.com

iCrew Digital Publishing is an independent publisher of digital works. We support the efforts of authors who wish to self- publish in the digital world.

Website for Jon P. Gunn

 Created with Vellum

www.ingramcontent.com/pod-product-compliance
Lightning Source LLC
Chambersburg PA
CBHW060929120626
46557CB00003B/927